The Life of
WOODY GUTHRIE

THERE AIN'T NOBODY THAT CAN SING LIKE ME

The Life of
WOODY GUTHRIE

THERE AIN'T NOBODY THAT CAN SING LIKE ME

by
Anne E. Neimark

ATHENEUM BOOKS FOR YOUNG READERS
New York London Toronto Sydney Singapore

Atheneum Books for Young Readers

An imprint of Simon & Schuster Children's Publishing Division

1230 Avenue of the Americas

New York, New York 10020

Book design by Anne Scatto

The text of this book is set in Minion.

Printed in the United States of America

First Edition

10 9 8 7 6 5 4 3 2 1

Library of Congress Cataloging-in-Publication Data

Neimark, Anne E.

There ain't nobody that can sing like me : the life of Woody Guthrie /
by Anne E. Neimark.

p.   cm.

Includes bibliographical references (p.) and index.

ISBN 978-1-5344-0950-7

1. Guthrie, Woody 1912–1967—Juvenile literature. 2. Folk singers—
United States—Bibliography—Juvenile literature. [1. Guthrie, Woody
1912–1967. 2. Singers. 3. Folk music.] I. Title.

Ml3930.G88 N45 2002

782.42162'13'0092—dc21

[B]   00-056933

To Jarrett Taylor Neimark–
A song of strength,
A song of love

I lived in a place called Okfuskee
And I had a little girl in a holler tree
I said, little girl, it's plain to see,
there ain't nobody that can
    sing like me

She said it's hard for me to see
how one little boy got so ugly
yes, my little girly, that might be,
but there ain't nobody that can
    sing like me
Ain't nobody that can sing like me,

Way over yonder in the minor key
Way over yonder in the minor key,
there ain't nobody that can
    sing like me

We walked down by the Buckeye
    Creek
to see the frog eat the goggle eye bee
To hear that west wind whistle to
    the east,
there ain't nobody that can
    sing like me

Oh my little girly will you let me see,
way over yonder where the wind
    blows free
Nobody can see in our holler tree
and there ain't nobody that can
    sing like me

Her mama cut a switch from a
    cherry tree
and laid it on the she and me,
It stung lots worse than a hive
    of bees
but there ain't nobody that can
    sing like me

Now I have walked a long long ways
and I still look back to my
    tanglewood days,
I've led lots of girls since then to
    stray
saying, ain't nobody that can
    sing like me

—"WAY OVER YONDER IN
THE MINOR KEY"

AUTHOR'S NOTE

Learning about Woody Guthrie was like discovering the rich vein of silver dreamed about by the Guthrie family after J. P. Guthrie, Woody's grandfather, staked out, then lost sight of, a silver mine in the south Texas mountains. Books, articles, essays, pamphlets, newspaper columns, songbooks (many of which were written by Woody himself), dozens of old phonograph records of his songs, and new audio cassettes, CDs, and a video provided a treasure trove of material.

Conversations with some of Woody's family members and friends, as well as with folks who were "there at the time," proved invaluable. Mary Jo Guthrie Edgmon (Woody's sister) opened her home and heart to me. Studs Terkel, author, broadcasting star, and former actor, regaled me with tales of "housing" Woody on his apartment floor during the week that Woody, Pete Seeger, Lee Hays, and Millard Lampell crashed an Illinois picket line of cotton strikers. Pete Seeger (who told me he never thinks of Woody without remembering "a flicker of a grin around the corners of his mouth") and Arlo Guthrie performed hours of soul-stirring folk music (salted with laughter)—the kind of honest tunes Woody loved—when I visited the annual folk festival honoring Woody's birthday in his hometown of Okemah, Oklahoma. I am also grateful to Nora Guthrie (Woody's daughter) and Harold Leventhal, director and executive trustee, respectively, of the Woody Guthrie Foundation and Archives in New York; to Judy Leventhal, head of the Woody Guthrie Publications in New York; to Don Moore, president of Okemah's Chamber of Commerce; to Okemah's Woody Guthrie Coalition; and to Thelma Bray, chairperson of the Pampa, Texas, annual tribute to Woody, for allowing me access to and/or use of "Woody material" and for answering so many of my questions.

What lingers most are the days I spent during the summers of 1999 and 2000 walking Okemah's streets, seeing what Woody saw. Not much has changed. I found his initials in the pavement by a flower shop, laughed over the potbellied water tower with his name printed on it in huge letters, gaped at his bronze statue on Main Street's tiny park, and attended a folk-music program at the Crystal Theatre, where Woody's mother found such comfort from pain. All of this was a kaleidoscope of shapes and colors, a still-living reminder of Guthrie tragedies and triumphs. Driving on Route 66, I could have said, "So long, Woody, it's been good to know you"—but I don't think we'll ever really say good-bye.

chapter ONE

Many a page of life has turned,
Many lessons I have learned,
I feel like in those hills I still
belong—
    —"OKLAHOMA HILLS"

Children of
a migrant family
on Oklahoma's
Highway 1, 1938

nother cyclone had ripped into the small town of Okemah, Oklahoma. Six-year-old Woody Guthrie remembered the winds "squealing like a hundred mad elephants." Knots of hay had been hurled onto the locust trees along Ninth Street, now hanging in wild, feathery gnarls from the branches. Roof shingles lay on the grass, spotted with manure from the barns. Doors had burst open and banged shut, splintering into pieces that flew over the pond along with dust, gravel, and uprooted weeds.

This latest windstorm caused nightmares in many Okemah children, scarier to Woody than the goosebump tales told to him by workers and drifters at the train yard. Yet on this May morning of 1919, two

Woody's parents,
Nora and Charley
Guthrie, circa 1908

days after the cyclone, calm had returned. Woody's mother, Nora, sat at the piano on the stone floor of their house, playing and singing Irish and English ballads. His father, Charley, and his older sister and two brothers—fourteen-year-old Clara, twelve-year-old Roy, and one-year-old George—were gathered at the piano.

How Woody loved music! His parents sang songs while they planted crops, fed the cows, or scrubbed the floors—old songs, they said, born in other lands or sprouting up among American rodeos, campfires, churches, and even prisons. Work songs, ballads, gospel tunes, cowboy verses. Nora Guthrie's bedtime lullabies were like a "nice ripe and juicey [*sic*] strawberry" to Woody, and he could find music anywhere. "There never was a sound," he would say, "that was not music—the splash of an alligator . . . the whistle of a train . . . a truck horn blowing . . . kids squawling [*sic*] along the streets." Music made everything "all plainer" to understand, even a scary cyclone.

When cyclones came, Woody's mother worried about the family's safety. But his father, who negotiated land deals between the white settlers and the local Native Americans (Choctaw, Cherokee, Chickasaw, Creeks, and Seminoles), was known as a tough fistfighter and refused to be scared. "Let the wind get harder," he'd shout to Woody. "Let the straw and feathers fly! Let the old wind go crazy and pound us over the head! And when the straight winds pass over and the twisting winds crawl in the air like a rattlesnake in boiling water, let's you and me holler back at it and laugh it back to where it come from!"

Now Nora Guthrie rose from the piano, shooing Roy off to school, taking George in her arms, and sending Woody to collect eggs from the hens. But Clara, a headstrong girl with light brown ringlets of hair, was told to stay home from school to do chores because she'd been unruly. Clara loudly objected, reminding her mother of a final exam required for graduation. Nora, however, would not relent. She'd been moody ever since her yellow dream house, built for the family by Charley's father, had suddenly burned down a month after it was finished. Although Charley served proudly as district court clerk for Okfuskee County (where Okemah lay), and successfully sold tenant farms and taught penmanship, Nora seemed fitful. Usually quiet, she'd started yelling at Charley about his fistfights with land sharks and politicians on the muddy, unpaved streets. Charley was popular with Okemah citizens, which had once pleased Nora, but now she resented his holding court each morning in Parsons' Drugstore. She preferred him to be home, talking to her or reading the law books and leather-bound classics he collected.

Several hours after Nora and Clara's argument, Woody was playing along Ninth Street when he heard the fire whistle blow. Its "song" always sounded sad to him, like some of his mother's ballads. With all the spooky talk between his parents about fire after the yellow house had turned to ashes, Woody ran home as fast as he could. Fire was worse than cyclones! In his yard he found tear-soaked neighbors and relatives; in his house a darkness made him shiver.

Clara, Woody learned, lay in bed—horribly burned. After the argument she'd poured coal oil on her dress and lit a match to frighten her mother. The oil had exploded, covering Clara in flames. Aghast, Nora watched her daughter stumble into the yard, screaming and crying. A neighbor wrapped Clara in blankets, smothering the flames, and carried her into the house. The doctor had come; Charley, Roy, and others had gathered. Clara's skin, Woody heard, was hanging off her body.

When he was allowed into the bedroom, he tiptoed forward in shadow, a wiry little boy, small for his age, with a mop of curly black hair. One of his uncles had said that naming the runt of the litter Woodrow Wilson Guthrie ("Woody" for short) was too burdensome a name for a boy, but Charley Guthrie, captivated by politics, had named his second son after the man nominated for president by the Democrats just a week before Woody's birth on July 14, 1912.

Woody stood beside Clara's bed, startled that she was smiling. "Hello there, old Mister Woodly," Clara said, using her pet name for him. Though her charred and blistered skin seemed unattached to her body, Clara's face was serene, her ringlets of hair bubbling across the pillow. No one, she said, not Woody nor the rest of the family, must worry. She would be up playing "in a day or two." Nothing was hurting her.

Woody could not have known that the burns had destroyed the nerve endings in Clara's body that signaled pain. "Everybody's cryin', Woody," Clara said. "Papa's in there with his head down crying. . . . Mama's in the dining room, crying her eyes out."

"I know," Woody said.

"Woodly," Clara whispered, "don't you cry. Promise me that you won't ever cry. It doesn't help, it just makes everybody feel bad, Woodly."

Nodding, Woody stood staunchly on the stone floor. There weren't any fires or cyclones just then. The winds had turned from mad elephants to mice, and Clara could smile. But that night, with not enough skin to protect her body, Clara gradually froze to death. She lay calmly on her bed like Sleeping Beauty, from the fairy tale. Before her eyes closed, she was visited by Mrs. Johnston, her schoolteacher, who told her—in answer to Clara's question—that, indeed, she *could* graduate with her class even though she had missed the exam.

The tragedy of fourteen-year-old Clara Guthrie's death would haunt the family forever, one of many misfortunes, as well as triumphs, that lay ahead. Charley Guthrie would always carry a photograph of his daughter in his pocket, tucked in an envelope on which he'd written MY LITTLE ANGEL. Woody would never forget his sister's bravery—or the promise he'd made her. He might not have been the biggest of six-year-old boys, but he was certainly big enough, he told himself, not to cry.

Woody (left) with his parents and younger brother, George, early 1920s

Although it was Clara who had died, Nora seemed, in her own way, to be disappearing. Townspeople blamed her for Clara's death, gossiping about her moodiness, saying she had lit Clara on fire. Nora roamed the streets, a tortured look in her eyes. She lost control of her muscles, and her arms swung like crazed pendulums; her gait was stiff and awkward. The times when she was her old self, singing to Woody, cooking, cleaning, planting flowers, he felt hopeful—but then a spell would seize her. She'd stop bathing and cry for days. Snarling at her children in a garbled voice, she broke furniture and dishes, and once, she rode a horse through town wearing only a slip, her dark hair a web of tangles. Clara's death, Woody would explain, was "a breaking point for my mother."

Woody and Roy cleaned up after Nora, trying to hide some of her oddness from their father. Woody loved Nora deeply, but he knew she was "all twisted out of shape" and no longer "just like any other boy's mama." Sometimes he went with her to movies at the Crystal Theatre on Main Street. In the musty darkness no one could stare at her. Nora even laughed when Charlie Chaplin, the actor, played the little tramp who, though a misfit, kept his funny, unsinkable optimism.

After his seventh birthday Woody began attending school, but he often played hooky. He poked around the train yard, his pants full of holes that Nora had forgotten to mend. Hoboes and drifters told him their own tales of woe. These down-and-outers, as they were called, didn't know about the Guthries' house burning down . . . or about Clara's death . . . or about Nora's sickness. So to Woody, they were safe.

Besides, too much was happening at home for anyone to keep tabs on him. Already depressed over Nora's behavior, Charley had lost an election for the state legislature and developed painful arthritis in his fistfighting hands. Bills piled up from taking Nora to local doctors, and Charley had to sell land and farms he owned to pay them. He didn't say much when talk at Parsons' Drugstore turned to the discovery of oil near Okemah.

Dazed, Charley watched thousands of "oil boomers" crash into town, their shacks spreading in the fields like dusty toadstools. Wagons with oil machinery rattled down the streets, and empty liquor bottles littered the churchyard and cemetery. The population of Okemah ballooned from two thousand to ten thousand in a matter of months. Okemah was making its mark, but Charley Guthrie, now forty-one years old and tainted by disaster, had become a has-been.

By 1923 Charley couldn't pay the rent on the house on Ninth Street. The year before, Nora had given birth to their fifth child—a girl named Mary Josephine (called "Tinkin" by Woody)—and in July 1923 Charley moved the family in a rusty Model T truck to Oklahoma City. He would make a new start, he vowed, and Nora would heal. She did seem to feel better in the ramshackle house they rented there. She swept, washed, cooked, even tied twine to the

The Guthrie birthplace in Okemah (photo taken in 1979)

window screens so that the sweet peas she'd planted could climb up. Her improvement, Woody would say, "looked like the front door of heaven to all of us."

Charley tried selling fire extinguishers, lugging them all over the city, but he earned little money. Though his arthritis made it painful to lift anything heavy, he took a delivery job at a grocery for one dollar a day. Roy helped out with odd jobs, and Woody earned a dollar a week from a lady with a cow by carrying milk to the store to be sold. Only "one or two sticks of furniture" were in the house, Woody would recall, and Charley's shoes were split. At night he'd ask Woody to rub his hands so he could sleep. When the arthritis caused the little finger on his left hand to fold down so tightly that it cut an oozing hole in his palm, a doctor amputated the finger.

Sadly, Charley said that he'd finally lost a fight. "You done good, Papa," Woody protested, rubbing his father's swollen fingers and remembering the old days in Okemah. "You decided what was good and you fought every day for it."

Good luck seemed to have finally arrived when Nora's half brother Leonard hired Charley as manager of his Ace Motorcycle Company. Excited, the Guthries danced around the house. "The world got twice as big and four times brighter," Woody would say. "Flowers changed colors, got taller, more of them." But one day later Leonard was killed in a crash between his motorcycle and a car. Solemnly, the family drove back to Okemah. The place they rented now was in the town's poorest section, a sagging house with rotted shingles and floorboards. The two rooms, lean-to kitchen, and porch had tin buckets to catch leaks. "Home sweet home," brother Roy remarked wryly to Woody, George, and Mary Jo.

Nora was relieved to have the Crystal Theatre to go to again, but her seizures returned. Syrups and powders from the doctors, who called her problem "hysteria," didn't help. She'd fall to the floor, her stomach knotting into lumps, saliva running from her mouth. Once, she chased five-year-old George around the house with a knife until he jumped out a window, and three-year-old Mary Jo was seen wandering alone in traffic.

Shaken by Nora's behavior, Charley found a job issuing auto licenses for Okfuskee County. Woody went back to school, though he rarely showed up; instead, he dragged a burlap sack across town, collecting throwaways to sell at the junkyard so Charley could keep buying medicine for Nora. His schoolmates made fun of him. At age thirteen he was still small, with frizzled hair and an Adam's apple in his neck that bobbed up and down when he spoke. "Scarecrow" and "Alley Rat," other kids called him. Hadn't his family been cursed by fire and death? Hadn't his father lost all his money? And wasn't his mother plumb crazy?

Nora's "craziness" may have been the reason why Charley, napping one Saturday night in June 1927, was severely burned across his chest from an oil lamp that Nora carried. He was rushed to the local hospital. Mary Jo and George, the youngest children, were sent to their aunt Maude's home in Texas, but Charley wouldn't blame his wife. He did agree, however, to recuperate at Maude's after he was released from the hospital.

Woody, frequently alone now, dirty and hungry as he neared his fifteenth birthday, would hitchhike to the farm outside Okemah owned by the Tanners, his grandparents on his mother's side. As Mary Tanner, his grandmother, cooked his lunch or dinner, she'd cry over Nora's collapse, over Clara's death and Charley's ghastly burns, over the grief that fire had caused the family. Finally, Claude Guthrie, Woody's uncle, drove out from where he lived in nearby Henryetta to see Nora. Stepping amid broken dishes and filth at the Guthrie house, he tried talking to her. When she offered to cook him eggs and threw the cracked shells into the pan, Claude took matters into his own hands.

That afternoon, whistling a tune his mother used to sing, Woody hitchhiked home from the Tanners' to find his house empty. Roy, he knew, was working odd jobs, but darting through the littered rooms, tripping over the tin buckets, Woody hunted for Nora. By sundown he learned that doctors had taken her away to the state insane asylum at Norman. He would, over time, be both wounded and toughened by this latest catastrophe. If boys from school dared make fun of his mother, he punched them in the nose with a strength he didn't know he had. What he did know was that he missed Nora dearly, but that he'd been missing her for a long time. Years would pass, however, before Woodrow Wilson Guthrie, his dead sister Clara's "Mister Woodly," would learn what had really been wrong with his mother—and its cruel destiny for the family.

chapter TWO

You've gotta walk that lonesome valley,
You gotta walk it by yourself,
Nobody here can walk it for you,
You gotta walk it by yourself.
 —"LONESOME VALLEY"

Homeless Oklahoma children bound for California, 1936

Bad memories leaked into the house like the rain in the dented tin buckets. Both Woody and Roy wanted to go away, but when Roy rented a room and asked his brother to join him, Woody refused. On a scruffy hill in town was an old shack where a dozen or so boys—oil boomers' kids—hung out. Woody dubbed the group a "gang" and himself the leader. He nailed the Ten Commandments, as if they were bylaws, to a mildewed wall and outlawed cussing. Taking a quilt, a blanket, and his burlap sack from the house, he moved into the lopsided shack.

Aside from digging "like a mole into everybody's trash heaps," he shined shoes and washed spittoons at the Broadway Hotel. He was still skipping school, his report card left unclaimed in the front office. A black shoe-shine boy gave him a harmonica and taught him to play the mournful sounds of "Railroad Blues," and if he was hungry, his grandparents or Mrs. Chowning, the banker's wife, would feed him. He stole a few quarts of milk from front porches before realizing he didn't need to be a petty thief. Having quickly mastered the harmonica, he could throw his cap on Main Street, play some tunes, dance a jig, and collect enough coins from passersby to buy food.

Woody lived in the shack for almost a year, his quilt moldy and torn, until the late winter of 1928. Sometimes he'd scare the other boys with wild tales about the loathsome creatures in the junkyard—"Half-kids and half-rats," he'd say, "half-coyotes and half-men." Or, just to stir up excitement, he'd swim across the lake with a rock tied around his neck. If he envied the boys for sleeping in real beds, with mothers and fathers nearby, he didn't let on. His father wrote him twice a week from Aunt Maude's in Texas, and he'd write back, sending notes to George and Mary Jo.

Finally winter's icy cold chilled him into fever and dizziness. He stumbled into Roy's rented room, where he lay on the bed for two days while his brother tended to him. When one of the gang boys, Casper

Man hopping a freight car in Bakersfield, California, 1940

THERE AIN'T NOBODY THAT CAN SING LIKE ME

Moore, said that his family would let Woody live with them, he decided to go.

Woody stayed at the Moores' until he was sixteen, at ease with Tom Moore, the father, who'd lost his money like Charley and who played the fiddle. With his harmonica Woody memorized old Tennessee hymns that Tom liked, and found he could make up new verses right on the spot. He played a Jew's harp, a small metal instrument held against the teeth and struck with the hand, and made music with combs, pencils, grass, water glasses, and bottles.

After he was fired from the Broadway Hotel for drawing cartoons on the menus, he was persuaded by Tom to return to school. Briefly he was joke editor for the yearbook and wrote for the school paper, but he quit when the Moores decided to move to Arizona. He wouldn't go with them, but he asked Tom to drive him sixty miles to Norman to see Nora at the asylum. The visit was unbearably grim. Locked away like an animal, shaking and hollow-eyed, Woody's mother didn't even recognize him. He fled down the corridors as the inmates grimaced or cackled at him. Outside the redbrick building he leaned over the hood of Tom's car and, unable to keep his promise to Clara never to cry, he sobbed.

With the Moores gone, Woody hit the road west from Okemah. He hitchhiked or hopped freight trains, sleeping under bridges or trees. In Houston and Galveston, Texas, and at the Gulf of Mexico, he hoed figs and picked grapes in orchards with thousands of migrant families. At campfires, underfed, barefoot children sat in his lap, and hard-luck stories circled around him from migrants who followed the harvests to the west and north like moths follow a flame. Returning to Okemah, he was hired at a gas station for five dollars a week. Roy was steadily employed at a local food store. Woody's stained shirts and rumpled overalls were a stark contrast to his brother's neatly ironed clothes.

One morning in 1929 Woody stopped at the post office and

picked up a letter from Charley. His father's chest burns, the letter said, were finally healing. He'd been able to take a job managing a rooming house in the oil-boom town of Pampa, Texas. Come and live with me, Charley urged. Lend me a hand.

Before the day was over, Woody had tossed his few belongings into a bag. He'd discovered that he liked not staying in one place. He didn't really care about making money—a pursuit that had whipped his father. If he had dollars crumpled in his overalls, he often gave them away, especially if he saw beggars on the street.

Yep, he told himself as he set off down the road toward Pampa, it was good-bye to Okemah—to the scrub oak and locust trees, the sand hills and prairies. Good-bye to the asylum at Norman. Farewell to all the weeds, those in the ground and those in his family, that he'd seen "sprout and grow, turn dry, go to seed, sprout and grow and turn dry again."

But Woody left one thing behind in Okemah: the initials WG, which he had carved into the newly laid concrete pavement on Main Street.

"Rooming house" was a fancy name for where Charley worked, a rambling, two-story building made of pine and corrugated tin, full of smells and secrets. It was filled with Pampa's oil boomers, who'd turned the sleepy farm community upside down.

Charley slept behind a curtain in a shabby office in the building. Most of the first floor was packed with cubicles holding cots; boomers rented them at twenty-five cents for eight hours—eating, boozing, sleeping, and paying extra for the mostly good-hearted prostitutes on the second floor. Woody helped his father collect the rents. The upstairs girls considered him, at seventeen, a kid, and he often did seem childlike, with his quiet spunk and devilish grin. He told jokes, made the girls giggle, and drew cartoons that he hung throughout the building.

He began working part-time at nearby Harris Drugstore, making sodas and banana splits. It didn't take him long to see that Shorty Harris, the owner, was really making his money selling liquor under the front counter. Shorty didn't fuss over Woody's work time or his plucking away on an old guitar he found in the back room. Woody waited on spiffed-up young men who came in for sodas and bragged about their future. He hadn't planned ahead; he figured the way life went, his future would run smack into fire or some other catastrophe.

One day that summer he found his father in a chair, weeping. "It's your mother, Woodrow," Charley said. "She died." Numbly, Woody read the letter from the asylum, with its check for $1.50, the balance of Nora's account. His mother had not been diagnosed at Norman as the usual hysteric. Apparently she'd suffered from a rare neurological disease, Huntington's chorea, which slowly destroys muscle capacity and brain cells. Woody deposited the check at the Pampa bank, then disappeared for a week.

Soon after his eighteenth birthday he slung the old guitar from Harris Drugstore over his shoulder and asked his father's half brother Jeff to teach him chords. Though Jeff lived in town with his wife, Allene, and worked for the police department, he yearned for a show business career. In Pampa he was known as a whiz on the guitar. Before long he and Woody were playing country songs, work and war songs, and dozens of black spirituals. Jeff was amazed at how quickly Woody learned. Neither of them liked the slick, big-city pop or band tunes on phonographs and jukeboxes. What touched them were songs of the workers, of pain and hope, passed along through generations by word of mouth. "Folk music," such songs were often called; many had come to America from England, Scotland, Ireland, and Africa. Over the years, words to the songs might have changed, but folk music kept its basic honesty. "Yankee Doodle," Jeff and Woody played. "John Brown's Body," "Barbara Allen," "All God's Children Got Shoes."

In his off hours from the drugstore and the rooming house, Woody began playing guitar and singing with Jeff at country fairs, barn dances, and hoedowns. He kept getting better at it. Like many of the folksingers he admired, he couldn't read music, but he played, he said, "by ear, by touch, by feel, by bluff, by guessin', by fakin', and by great crave and drive to keep on playing."

With another guitarist, named Cluster Baker, and a new friend, Matt Jennings, he formed the Corncob Trio. Red-haired, freckled, and shy, Matt was one of three children from a poor Irish-Catholic family. He was energized by Woody, and knowing that his friend's favorite "talking" was music, he'd bought himself a pawnshop guitar and learned to play it. Woody painted signs advertising the group and tacked them on telephone poles. He talked Matt into letting the trio practice at the Jenningses' dilapidated cottage. A small but steady audience would gather—neighbors, family members, and their most devoted listener, blond-haired Mary Jennings, Matt's fourteen-year-old sister.

The Corncob Trio hoped their music would survive the pop-tune craze in Pampa. Folk music had been ignored by most record companies, but now radio was making inroads into rural areas with its folk broadcasts. To compete, several record companies recorded folk artists, and two stars appeared on the national scene: Mississippi's Jimmie Rodgers, who could yodel so expertly that lines formed at stores for his records, and Virginia's singing Carter family—A. P. Carter; his wife, Sara; and sister-in-law Maybelle.

One Saturday night, strolling with Mary Jennings from a dance where the Corncob Trio had entertained, Woody hesitantly put a hand on her shoulder. She blushed but moved closer. Telling a few jokes, he started a game he'd played with his father in Okemah, changing the order of word combinations to make them verbal commands. *Sunbeam* became "Beam, sun!" Mary laughed, and then there was no stopping him. *Rainstorm* was "Storm, rain!"; *groundswell* was

"Swell, ground!" He'd been scrambling words into several songs of his own, writing them down on paper napkins, fooling with their spelling. "Manhandled ya, egg scrambled ya, spondoolyzed ya," he said to Mary. She seemed delighted. Woody Guthrie was not at all like the other boys in Pampa.

In 1932, at age twenty, Woody asked Mary Jennings to marry him. Although she was only fifteen, she said yes. Woody realized how lonely he'd been since Nora died, and that Mary never seemed to look at him like he was a freak. Together, they asked Mary's father, Harry Jennings, for his blessing. Harry had taken a shine to *that Guthrie fellow,* as he was known among the Jenningses, especially when Woody sang "When You Wore a Tulip," but he was outraged at the idea of marriage for his teenage daughter. Woody wasn't even Catholic, didn't have a good enough job or future prospects, and couldn't keep a dime in his pocket. "Absolutely not!" Harry Jennings said.

Woody kept his cool. He didn't talk back, but didn't give up. He told himself that marrying Mary was a hold-your-horses situation. It was a "take it easy," like when you wrote a song with a melody in mind, knowing what you wanted to say, but needing to keep trying to get it right. He decided it was only a matter of turning things around, making them different. Until then, he would just keep "groovin' it, greazin' it, dreamin' it, schemin' it." And then, Woody was sure—in the blink of an eye or in the eye of a blink—everything would be okay.

chapter THREE

You just keep a lamp lit for me. . . . You just keep
   a door key for me.
You just keep a little place for me.
And I'll take and rest my new head in a pallet
   down on your floor.
    I'll lay down.
And dream out a new kind of twist.
   —"BORN TO WIN"

Migrant family leaving Ioabel, Oklahoma, 1938

The marriage took place on October 28, 1933, at Holy Souls Cathedral Church in Pampa. No family members were present; the two witnesses were friends of Mary's who were at church that day. The newlyweds first rented a room above Jeff Guthrie's apartment, then moved into a drab cottage on Russell Street, near Mary's parents. Woody didn't feel like a kid anymore—not with a wife on his arm—but he didn't see himself as one of those tie-wearing, bring-home-the-bacon-every-Friday kind of guys, either.

Dozens of notions flew at him. He considered being a lawyer, and when he wasn't practicing with the trio, he read the law books Charley had brought to Pampa, dragging Mary down to the courthouse each morning to hear the latest case. But he lost interest in lawyering when he read about adobe houses, made of clay and unable to burn down. He considered building them in Texas, but when instructions arrived in the mail, he discovered that Pampa didn't have the right clay content in its soil.

Mary was charmed but a little overwhelmed by her new husband. She kept busy by typing up the romance stories he tried his hand at, as well as the new songs he'd written. He sent them off to magazines and song publishers, where they were politely rejected. Undaunted, Mary talked to other customers at Harris Drugstore or the food market about the Corncob Trio appearing on weekends at the Tokyo Bar or on a Pampa radio show.

Woody sometimes liked keeping things private, and he didn't tell Mary, his father, or Matt Jennings that the local librarian, Mrs. Todd, had encouraged him to read books in Pampa's library, which was nestled in the basement of City Hall. Drawn to the volumes on spirituality, mysticism, and the occult, he became fascinated with the Bible and Kahlil Gibran's *The Prophet.* Matt Jennings's eyes grew wide when Woody, if he wanted to, quoted from the Bible as accurately as the town preacher.

When food was scarce or the rent due, Woody used his talent at drawing cartoons to earn money painting signs. He started painting landscapes, animals, even heads of Jesus on canvas, but buyers were few. A sign he painted on Harris Drugstore drew praise, however, so he began painting signs for other stores, for warehouses, hotels, and restaurants, for hockshops and funeral parlors. He mailed ideas for signs to big companies and received, even in the midst of the financial depression that had hit the country in 1929, job offers he ignored.

Oil paintings and signs, even if they "lasted a thousand years," were never as important to Woody as songs. A song, he'd say, was a conversation "fixed up to where you can talk it over and over without getting tired of it. And it's repeating the idea over and over again that makes it take a hold." Songs, Woody said, could give comfort and fire up people to make the world better. He always got a lump in his throat, remembering Nora, when he heard the words to the old black spiritual "Sometimes I Feel Like a Motherless Child."

His guitar from Harris Drugstore had become like another limb on his body. It was the guitar, not Mary, that lay next to him when he slept some nights at the Tokyo Bar after playing for patrons until they went home. Mary, he told himself, would understand. And on predawn mornings when he slipped into the house from the sticky blackness of the train yard, it was his guitar that had "talked" to drifters waiting to hop freights illegally. Many down-and-outers were searching desperately for jobs during the financial depression of the 1930s, often abandoning their wives and children. Some, like Charley, had successfully traded plots of land, but depression or drought had ruined them. Woody saw a decency in these men; they weren't the useless riffraff, or rubbish, that people called them.

Charley had left the rooming house after Woody's wedding, having already surprised the family by marrying one of the mail-order brides advertised in a magazine. Bettie Jean McPherson of Los Angeles was a hefty woman who practiced fortune-telling, healing, tarot cards, dream symbols, and palmistry. Charley had rented them a cheap tourist-court cottage, and Bettie Jean advertised for customers in the local paper. When the family met Bettie Jean, they guessed from her scowls that she might have a mean streak. Everyone was wary of the union, except for Woody. Here was someone who practiced the very things he'd read about in Pampa's library! He overlooked some of the harsh comments Bettie Jean made to Charley and even treated some of her leftover clients with his own fortune-telling. But he never charged a penny for his services.

The youngest Guthrie, Mary Jo, now nine years old, and George, who was five, were brought to live with their papa and Bettie Jean at the cottage, and Woody excitedly visited them. He chalked up the paleness in their faces to their leaving Aunt Maude. He couldn't stop talking about a trip he'd taken into south Texas with his father, his brother Roy, and Jeff to look for a silver mine that his grandfather Jerry P. Guthrie had found at a mountain spring. With J. P.'s crudely drawn maps to guide them, the four Guthries had rattled down Route 66 in a dented truck. Woody played guitar all along the Rio Grande and into the Chisos Mountains. The trip proved fruitless, of course, since thousands of mountain springs dotted the area, but Woody had been struck by the awesome majesty of the land.

One evening while he was eating supper at the court, he heard Mary Jo complain about a math test scheduled at her school. She looked unhappy, he thought—skittery and fearful, which wasn't her nature. Using what he'd read in Bettie Jean's palmistry books, he hunkered down by Mary Jo's bed after she fell asleep. Taking her small hand in his, he blocked out the noise of clanging pots and

Dust storm from Oklahoma and Texas

muttering in Bettie Jean's kitchen, concentrating on transmitting into Mary Jo's mind, from somewhere in the great unknown, the answers to the test.

Days later Woody told everyone that Mary Jo had passed the math test with flying colors. He was, however, still worried about her. Something was wrong. Only when Roy—who'd married and now lived with his wife, Ann, in Konawa, Oklahoma—actually "kidnapped" Mary Jo out of Bettie Jean's clutches and brought her to his house did Woody learn the truth. For no reason at all, Bettie Jean McPherson Guthrie had been beating his sister with a sharp-bristled hairbrush, then forcing her to wash away her tears so his father wouldn't notice.

The irony, Woody realized, was that Mary Jo's favorite posses-sion was another hairbrush, one with soft bristles and a shiny wooden handle, which had belonged to their dead sister, Clara. Per-haps, Woody thought, Mary Jo also felt "like a Motherless Child."

Drawing by
Woody Guthrie

In 1935, when Woody was twenty-three years old, the entire country seemed tired and flat. Twenty mil-lion people were out of work. Many had lost their savings in the depres-sion's stock market crash. People stood by the thousands in bread lines, waiting for handouts of food. In his Fireside Chats on radio, Pres-ident Franklin D. Roosevelt prom-ised a New Deal to provide jobs for the unemployed—public works projects like those administered by the WPA (Works Progress Admin-istration).

Woody didn't have cash to lose and didn't really want a steady job. He still gave away dollars to beggars—even if Mary was waiting at home to pay bills. He knew Mary's parents doubted he'd ever be able to support their daughter, but he couldn't stomach the prospect of a nine-to-five job. Instead, he put fourteen songs he'd written into a typed booklet and chose a zany title: *Alonzo M. Zilch's Own Collection of Original Songs and Ballads.* Despite the title, his songs didn't kid around. "If I Was Everything on Earth" spoke to the plight of the poor, the government's prohibition of liquor, and the pollution of water by the oil industry:

> If I was President Roosevelt,
> I'd make the groceries free—
> I'd give away new Stetson hats,
> And let the whiskey be.
> I'd pass out suits of clothing
> At least three times a week—
> And shoot the first big oil man
> That killed the fishing creek.

In February, Mary discovered she was pregnant. There would be another mouth to feed, but Woody wasn't going to worry about it. He'd sing, he told himself, at a few more gigs and paint more signs. He and Jeff had already chalked up enough musical experience to have been hired, two years back, by Texas rancher Claude Taylor for a traveling music show. And even though Taylor had called off the show several months later, after Mary and Alene, Jeff's wife, joined the troupe, hadn't everyone had fun cavorting in Texas towns?

But all of a sudden a new disaster hit the country. On April 14, 1935, the states of Oklahoma and Texas were covered by a vast shroud of dust that blew in from drought-ridden Nebraska and the

Dakotas. The dust storm, far more horrendous than the smaller dirt storms that frequently blew across the southwest, devoured houses, leaving clumps of dirt everywhere. Birds fell to the ground, laden with silt, and small animals dropped in their tracks. Many families locked themselves indoors, certain that the end of the world had arrived.

Woody and Mary, coughing from dust, could not lift the dark in their cottage by candle or lightbulb. With wet cloths over their faces, eyes stinging, they waited for morning. When it came, the storm had abated—but dust had suffocated grasslands and crops. No harvests could be shipped from the two panhandle states to the rest of the nation. A Washington, D.C., reporter dubbed both Texas and Oklahoma the Dust Bowl, a name that would enter history books.

Mortgages that couldn't be paid forced the foreclosures by banks of thousands of farms and houses. Parents bundled up their children and tied movable belongings to car tops (if they had a car) or onto their backs. Devastated but hoping to survive, they set off by car, foot, or freight for Arizona or California. Their pasts had collapsed behind them like deflated balloons, but folded in their pockets were crafty handbills distributed across the Dust Bowl by California landowners. COME TO CALIFORNIA! the handbills said. GOOD JOBS! STEADY PAY! HELP US PICK OUR RIPE STRAWBERRIES, PEACHES, AND CORN.

The brightest event for the Guthries that November was when Mary gave birth to Gwendolyn Gail, nicknamed "Teeny." To celebrate her birth, Woody wrote a lullaby called "Curly-Headed Baby." But he wasn't any more prepared for the responsibilities of fatherhood than he had been for marriage. Teeny was adorable—he changed her diapers and sang to her—but it soon felt like dust was choking him again. Sleeping out nights in a stranded railroad car, he was as isolated as he'd been at the gang house in Okemah. He watched dejected families trudging down Route 66, aching to join them. They were moving on, weren't they, going someplace new, while he was tied down in Pampa?

Mary's father had a talk with him about dependability, but he fidgeted through it. Arguing with Mary over nothing, making up, arguing again, he was an arrow already on its uncharted course. Leaving his tiny daughter in Mary's care, he hitched rides down the highway, visited his brother Roy in Konawa, and stayed a weekend with his father in Fort Smith, Arkansas, where Charley was making a last attempt to sell real estate. As he fled from Pampa he wrote down songs about the great dust storm of 1935.

One song kept somersaulting in his mind during his escapes from Mary and Teeny. Eventually, it would be published, recorded, and revised, becoming a great American classic. It captured in words some of what Woody wanted to say about breaking free:

SO LONG, IT'S BEEN GOOD TO KNOW YOU
(excerpts from two versions)

(1935 version)
I've sung this song, but I'll sing it again,
Of the place that I lived on the wild, windy plains,
In the month called April, the country called Gray,
And here's what all of the people there say:

So long, it's been good to know ye,
So long, it's been good to know ye,
So long, it's been good to know ye,
This dusty old dust is a getting my home,
And I've got to be drifting along.

(1950 version)

I've sung this song, but I'll sing it again,
Of the people I've met and the places I've been,
Of some of the troubles that bothered my mind,
And a lot of good people that I've left behind,
saying:

So long, it's been good to know ye,
So long, it's been good to know ye,
So long, it's been good to know ye,
What a long time since I've been home,
And I've got to be drifting along.

chapter FOUR

*I never did make up many songs about
the cow trails or the moon skipping
through the sky, but at first it was
funny songs of what's all wrong, and
how it turned out good or bad.
Then I got a little braver and made up
songs telling what I thought was wrong
and how to make it right.*

—BOUND FOR GLORY

Migrant child in front of "tent" in Harlingen, Texas, 1939

Woody called himself itchy footed. In other towns, other cities, he came upon those who'd been pushed down, knocked down, shoved down, and he saw their grit and courage. They might be dirt poor, they might not own much, the way rich people did, but they worked hard for what they did have. Hard was a word biting at the blisters on their feet. Hard traveling. Hard times.

The more Woody hitched rides, his paintbrushes in his pocket, his guitar strapped on his back, the longer Mary had to fend for herself and Teeny. He kept coming back to her, kept reviving the Corncob Trio, but there was no guarantee he'd show up. He would hoist Teeny onto his shoulders, but his spirit

Field worker picking cotton in San Joaquin, California, 1938

seemed left on the road. One day when Jeff and Allene were visiting, and he and Jeff were harmonizing on their guitars while Mary and her mother were cooking, Woody suddenly stood up and said, "Well, I'm going."

"Going," Jeff replied. "Where?"

"California," Woody said—and he meant right then and there. No one in the house could change his mind, and he was gone with a wave.

California would teach Woody more about the differences between the rich and poor, about hardship and survival, about politicians, law enforcers, and tycoons. In California, where fields and orchards were "such a thick green garden of fruits and vegetables that I didn't know if I was dreaming or not," he and the five hundred thousand migrant workers who'd poured into the state during the depression were scathingly called "Okies" or "poor white trash." Living under any sort of covering—paper bags, junkyard metal, leaves—the migrants, if they were lucky enough to find work, were exploited by landowners who hired them to pick crops.

Woody drifted from town to town, hopping freights. He'd drop down from the top of an open boxcar onto the machinery or bags of cement inside. He rode with as many as sixty ragged, out-of-work men—some crippled from heatstroke or injury, some old, some young—everyone cramped together like decaying sardines. Often he'd be asked to play something "good an' hot" on his guitar.

In Bakersfield he slept under railroad bridges and in doorways. In Sonoma he picked up loose change by painting signs for a store owner, sent postcards to Mary, and rented a flophouse cot for twenty-five cents. "If it had cockroaches, alligators, or snapping turtles in it," he said, "I was too sleepy to stay awake and argue with them." The police might run him out of town or jail him for the night. They sneered if he said he was looking for work. "Git on outta town!" they'd yell. "Keep travelin'! Don't you ever look back!"

When he first approached the California border, his greatest shock had been to see Los Angeles police forming an illegal roadblock and using billy clubs to stop migrants from entering the state. Even children were treated like vermin. Woody had written songs on the road, and his plain language gave a voice to the migrants' misery and blew the whistle on what had been done to them:

DO RE MI
Lots of folks back east, they say,
Leavin' home every day,
Beatin' the hot old dusty way
To the California line.

Cross the desert sands they roll,
Getting out of that old dust bowl,
They think they're going to a sugar bowl
But here's what they find:
Oh, if you ain't got the do re mi, folks,
If you ain't got the do re mi,
Why you better go back to beautiful Texas,
Oklahoma, Kansas, Georgia, Tennessee.
California is a garden of Eden,
A paradise to live in or see,
But believe it or not you won't find it so hot,
If you ain't got the do re mi.

A destitute family in migrant camp near Sacramento, California, 1936

BLOWIN' DOWN THIS ROAD

I'm blowin' down this old dusty road,
I'm blowin' down this dusty road,
I'm blowin' down this old dusty road, Lord God,
And I ain't a-gonna be treated this a-way.

I'm gonna change this damned old world around,
I'm gonna change this damned old world around,
I'm gonna change this damned old world around,
    Lord God,
And I ain't a-gonna be treated this way.

A movement had been taking root across the country to unionize workers, to guarantee them decent wages and fair treatment. Yet Woody saw that unionizing was still in "the nickel and the penny stages." In the late 1880s, the American Federation of Labor (AFL) had been formed. Then, in the early 1890s, came both the Socialist Party of the U.S. and the Industrial Workers of the World (IWW, nicknamed the "Wobblies"). The IWW were the rabble-rousers of the fledgling union movement, leading fierce but mostly futile strikes in Lawrence, Kansas; Massachusetts; and Spokane, Washington. While AFL president Samuel Gompers had said that what he wanted for workers was simply "More," and the Socialist Party had advocated worker pride, the CIO was now suggesting that unions be formed for whole industries, rather than by separate crafts. Unions, however, were a threat to many fruit growers.

Union leaders in California were often bullied, beaten up, or murdered by hired thugs and vigilantes. At union meetings around campfires, tear-gas bombs might explode. It was risky to filch even one orange or peach (even if you were starving) from fruit left to rot by growers who hoped to raise prices by reducing supplies.

Children of depression refugees went hungry while other ranchers sprayed gasoline on their fruit and burned it, and dairy farmers dumped thousands of gallons of milk into ditches.

Desperate workers finally marched in protest in Washington, D.C., demanding jobs through the public works programs. Strikes exploded in Los Angeles's aircraft industry, in Detroit's auto industry, and in other midwestern and eastern cities. But the gap between the haves and the have-nots in America—so agonizingly wide—would continue dividing loyalties and destroying lives.

One afternoon in 1938 Woody jumped from a freight car chugging through Redding, California. He'd heard on the road that a telegram was expected in Redding from Washington, D.C., authorizing work on a dam at the Sacramento River. Though not more than two thousand men would be hired, a camp of eight thousand migrants and their families already filled the adjacent fields. No official word, however, had arrived from Washington.

As he hiked into the camp, Woody saw a kind of catch-as-catch-can ghetto, women stirring watery soup in chipped jars, half-naked children crawling under cardboard boxes, men hammering or digging for worms. Apple crates, gunnysacks, and torn clothing had been nailed together into lean-to shelters; rusted car fenders, yanked up from junkyards, were wired to tree limbs as "umbrellas" or roofs. The camp reflected a sense of both worry and hope, pasted together like paper cutouts.

Woody walked past hundreds of families, patting the heads of their children. "Howdy," he'd say. "What's your name?" Flies, gnats, mosquitoes, roaches, and fleas were everywhere. He knew that the sacred word in migrant camps was *work*—just to have a job, to feed the kids, to put a smile on the wife's face. Any country, Woody would say, should take care of its poor folks and sick folks, not leave them "stuck in a tar pit of blind worries."

At sundown, under a tree, he played his guitar for the migrants, and a huge group gathered around him. People yelled out song titles from their hometown, wherever those might be, and he sang. With the moon shining on his mop of black hair, and his shirt and pants soiled with grease, Woody also sang some of his own songs—about the Dust Bowl, about hard luck and hard-get-by. His message that night gave faith that "we'll come through all of these [things] in pretty good shape, and we'll be all right, we'll work, we'll make ourselves useful—if only the telegram to build the dam would come in from Washington."

At dawn Woody was on his way. He'd never forget the camp in Redding or the brutality toward the migrants that he'd seen in California. But it was time, he knew—past time, actually—to go home to Mary. The fly in the ointment was his itchy feet. He was sure that once he got home, he'd again get the gnawing feeling that he should be "everywhere in the world except right [there]."

Women grappling with a National Guardsman at a strike in Gastonia, North Carolina, 1929

The only change in the cottage on Russell Street was another baby being inside. Woody and Mary now had a second daughter, Carolyn Sue (shortened to Sue). The Jennings in-laws, including Matt, shook their heads over Woody. He wasn't taking responsibility for his family. In the future he'd talk of "restless unrest," but for now he kept silent.

He showed a steely defiance, however, in the face of their disapproval. Sometimes he left notes for Mary saying he was going back on the road again (for a week, a month?), though other times he slipped away without notice. He made several more hitch-hiking trips to California and, in Glendale, looked up a cousin, Jack Guthrie, who played "gittar" and sang. Like Jeff Guthrie in Pampa, Jack worshiped show business. The big demand, he told Woody, was for singing cowboys like Chicago's Gene Autry, who yodeled as well as Jimmie Rodgers, or Leonard Slye (who took the name Roy Rogers). Jack bought himself a fancy cowboy outfit, asked Woody to be his sidekick, and—after some fast practicing—got them a job in a vaudeville show. When he convinced Frank Burke, owner of radio station KFVD in Los Angeles, to audition them, Woody quit washing dishes at Strangler Lewis's restaurant in Glendale.

KFVD hired Woody and Jack, but as the exposure alone was sup-posed to bring them jobs, they weren't paid anything. "Keep smil-ing!" was the tone of Woody's letters to Mary. "Before long, you'll be traveling out here to stay." He'd been writing new songs, and along with his and Jack's renditions of cowboy ballads like "Roundup Time" and "I'm an Old Cow Hand," he sang his own songs on the air. A friend of Jack's, Maxine Crissman (who had a nice, husky voice) was soon singing with him on KFVD, and Jack, nervous about money, went back to working full-time in construction.

Woody called Maxine, who was left-handed, "Lefty Lou." They received such a flood of mail from listeners, some with dollar bills inside, that Frank Burke soon gave them three radio shows a day. People wanted the words to Woody's songs, so he began mimeo-graphing and selling them for twenty-five cents each. In letters sent to Mary and his family he was so positive about Los Angeles and Glendale (where he'd rented a room) that his brother George left Oklahoma and moved out there.

At last, Frank Burke wrote his two "hillbilly stars" a contract for twenty dollars a week, plus commissions for signing up any new sponsors. Woody and Lefty Lou were especially popular with "countryfied" radio audiences in backwoods, mountain, and farm communities. Woody spun tales on the air and gave his opinions on everything from fried eggs to politics. "His people," as he called them, were tickled by his frequent jabs at the rich, and at "tie-coons" and "poly-tish-ens." Although he could speak and write with impressive grace, he used a country style on the show, coupled with his old game of playing with words. Lots of *ain'ts* and *cain'ts* speckled his sentences.

Along the nightlife strip in Los Angeles he bought beers and helped hard luckers in nearly every saloon "that had a [lit-up] neon sign." Finally he sent for Mary and the girls. To the dismay of the Jennings family, Mary swallowed her doubts about Woody and took the train to Los Angeles with Teeny and Sue. She wasn't surprised when Woody was two hours late picking them up. "Sorry, got lost," he said with childlike simplicity. He took everyone to the beach, where they collected seashells and he tumbled in the waves with the girls.

Woody worked at KFVD through most of 1939, except for a short stint at a station in Tijuana, Mexico. He and Lefty Lou put out four hundred booklets of twenty-four songs and various "Woodified" jokes called *Old Time Hill Billy Songs—Been Sung for Ages, Still Goin' Strong*. He became friendly with Ed Robbin, who had been hired for a radio spot by KFVD owner Frank Burke even though Ed was a raise-your-eyebrows liberal and the West Coast correspondent for *People's World,* a Communist Party newspaper. At first Ed regarded Woody as KFVD's uneducated country rube. But after talking to him, he found Woody to be smart, well read, and immensely talented.

Ed and Woody discovered their mutual goal—to get a fair

shake for America's working class—as did Ed's friend, actor Will Geer (who would play the grandfather on the TV series *The Waltons*). Union organizers whom Woody met with Ed and Will were a tireless, die-hard group. Usually members of the Communist Party, the dominant party in Russia since 1917, they believed that wealth should be shared among the lower, middle, and upper social classes. "From each according to his ability," said the party slogan, "to each according to his need." Though he never joined the party, Woody admired its ideals—never imagining in the 1930s, in the depths of the depression, that, by the 1950s, Communism would be considered a world oppressor by many Americans.

Woody and Will appeared together at picket lines and migrant camps, performing songs or doing readings. Woody was something of an Okie celebrity; he sang for "cotton pickers and cotton strikers, and for migratory workers, packers, canning house workers, fruit pickers, and all sorts of other country and city workers." Ed got him a tiny, spill-your-thoughts column in *People's World,* called "Woody Sez," and brought him to talk and sing at union halls, left-wing debates, fund-raisers, and picnics.

Woody and Mary Jennings Guthrie with their children Gwen, Sue, and Will (Bill)

After listening to various Communist Party leaders—Elizabeth Gurley Flynn, Blackie Meyers, William Z. Foster, Mother Bloor—Woody would saunter onto the stage, take a cigarette from his mouth, and tuck it into his guitar strings. Then, looking like a thin, scruffy boy, he'd sing—and talk politics—and sing—and sing. And within five or ten minutes the audience would be cheering. One of it's favorite Woody songs was "The Ballad of Pretty Boy Floyd":

Now as through this world I ramble
I've seen lots of funny men.
Some will rob you with a six gun
And some with a fountain pen.

Political talk in the U.S. grew noisier when Germany's Adolph Hitler invaded Poland in September 1939, setting the scene for World War II. Communists in America gasped in disbelief over Russia's nonaggression pact with the German dictator. In October of the same year, in the drab room in

Workers striking at an automobile factory

Glendale where Woody's two daughters played in his lap while he wrote songs, Mary gave birth to her third child and first son, Will Rogers Guthrie. Woody named the boy after the famous American humorist. Unfortunately, he'd missed his son's birth because he had been singing about peace at a union-backed strike in Arvin, California.

Wherever and whenever he performed, Woody felt "like a lost man getting found." His songs often asked questions about why harmful things were happening in the world. His answers, given through the musical poetry of his verses, suggested how human beings could stop what was harmful from ever happening again. Yet, at times, his unrest and his passion for song blotted out almost everything else in his life and hurt those who most loved and needed him. It was not always easy for Woody to follow his own advice.

chapter **FIVE**

My name is New York, I've been struck by the winds,

Froze up and blistered then struck down again;

Been struck by my rich folks,

Struck by my bums,

Been struck by my mansions, been struck by my slums.

I've been hit with diseases and troubles and pains;

I've seen my kids die under cartwheels and trains;

I smell the smoke roll, when it rolls from some hole

Where some cigarette spark takes a hundred good souls.

—"MY NAME IS NEW YORK"

PUNCHIN' TH' CLOCK

oody's radio show on KFVD gradually ran out of steam. Lefty Lou quit performing after she fell in love with a mechanic, and though Woody carried on as a lone wolf, the show started playing second fiddle to the political arguments he'd been having with Frank Burke. Frank had soured on Communism after Russia's 1939 pact with Hitler, while Woody was still a supporter. When the hatchet couldn't be buried, Woody left not only KFVD, but California as well, and decided to see what he could stir up in New York City, where Will Geer was appearing in a Broadway play, *Tobacco Road*.

He deposited Mary and the children back in Pampa after driving them across the desert in a broken-down car he'd bought. Scurrying away to Konawa, he visited his brother Roy and sister Mary Jo, sold Roy the car for thirty-five dollars, and hitched his way to New York. Will Geer and his wife, Herta, had an apartment on Fifty-ninth Street, where Woody slept on the couch.

The glitter and wealth of the city stunned him. When he learned that Will's apartment rented for $150, he thought that "that was for a whole year," not per month. He stared up at the majestic Empire State Building and newly built Rockefeller Center, but he also went down to the Bowery where drunks slumped against tavern walls, walk-up apartments had broken windows and rats that bit babies, and punks and criminals cruised the streets, kicking at homeless men. Woody saw that suffering was the same everywhere—caused by the same oppression—even in the great city of New York. Families from his home state of Oklahoma, their farms lost to bankers, their hopes for California shattered by false promises, were no different from people crouched on Bowery fire escapes, ill from the stench of urine in grubby hallways.

Will Geer put Woody on stage at various union lodges and at a gathering of Spanish refugees in New York's Mecca Temple. Audiences were first startled, then entranced, by the frankness of Woody's inspiring songs. The reedy, haunting twang of his voice prickled the hairs on the backs of their necks.

He would meet a number of people in New York who would become linchpins in his life. One was twenty-year-old Pete Seeger, a Harvard dropout who played banjo and shared Woody's respect for the downtrodden. Woody called him the "long tall stringbean [sic] kid from up in New England." Two friends, Ina and Bob Wood, who'd set up the Communist Party branch office in Oklahoma, gave Woody use of their typewriter. "They made me see," he'd say, "why I had to keep going around and around with my guitar making up songs and singing." Cisco Houston, a tenor who sang with Woody in California, became his friend, as did New

York City's black songwriter-guitar player and ex-convict from Louisiana, Huddie Ledbetter—known among fellow convicts as "Leadbelly."

Will Geer organized a benefit show at New York's Forrest Theater and asked Woody to be a headliner. Sparked by author John Steinbeck's 1939 novel *The Grapes of Wrath*, a story about the plight of migrant workers in America, Geer's show was a landmark in bringing traditional folk music to sophisticated urban audiences. The 1940 production would change the course of folk music in America, carrying it into big cities, and would introduce Woody to Alan Lomax, the man who finally brought him mainstream popularity.

New York had never seen the likes of Woody Guthrie—a political hillbilly, a hayseed minstrel with a mind like quicksilver. He had a repertoire of songs that could fill up hundreds of lonely nights, songs he'd heard and memorized and songs he'd written. The gritty "Union Maid" was created on Ina and Bob's typewriter, and became a favorite at hundreds of picket lines across the country. Woody said he wrote the song for a female union organizer who was stripped naked, beaten up, and hung from the rafters of a house:

> There once was a union maid who never was afraid
> Of the goons and ginks and company finks,
> And the deputy sheriffs who made the raids.
> She went to the union hall where a meeting it was called
> And when the company boys came 'round
> She always stood her ground . . .
>
> Oh you can't scare me, I'm sticking to the union,
> Sticking to the union, sticking to the union,
> Oh you can't scare me, I'm sticking to the union
> Sticking to the union, till the day I die.

Woody and Pete Seeger decided to sing songs and talk their talk on a trip through the Southwest. Driving in another old car that Woody bought, they stayed awhile with Mary and the children; saw Woody's father, who'd split up with Bettie Jean and now lived in Oklahoma City; and sang in saloons and for the Hooversville Camptowners' Community Camp on "the rim of Oklahoma's worst garbage dump."

Oklahoma migrant family bound for Oregon, 1937

Before the southwest trip, Woody had been cornered by Alan Lomax, who was dazzled listening to him perform. Lomax, assistant director of the Archive of Folksong at the Library of Congress in Washington, D.C., believed he'd discovered a treasure in Woody, a radical folk prophet from grass-roots America. He brought him to Washington and recorded hours of their conversations, sparked, as Woody recalled, by "all of the songs I could remember on a pint of pretty cheap whiskey." Twenty-five years would pass, however, before the Library of Congress recordings were made available to the public in a three-record set.

Influenced by Lomax's fervor over Woody, RCA Victor Records produced two albums of his Dust Bowl ballads, including "Dust Pneumonia Blues," "Dust Bowl Refugees," "I Ain't Got No Home in This World Anymore," and "Dust Can't Kill Me." RCA Victor had asked him to compose a *Grapes of Wrath* song, which he did in one night, naming it "Tom Joad" after Steinbeck's main character. The Dust Bowl albums, first popular at left-wing schools and camps, would eventually be considered twentieth-century masterpieces in music.

CBS Radio hired Woody to perform on *Back Where I Come From,* a new folk music show scheduled for prime time. With Lead-belly and folksinger Aunt Molly Jackson, he sang on WNYC, New

York's public radio station. And more success followed: CBS put him on their popular show *We, the People*, and appointed him host for the weekly show *Pipe Smoking Time*, using "So Long, It's Been Good to Know You" as the theme song. NBC Radio had him write and perform a ballad about Wild Bill Hickok for DuPont's *Cavalcade of America* show. In Woody's "blink of an eye," his earnings jumped to $350 per week, at least ten times what he'd been paid at KFVD in California.

Giddily, he sent again for Mary and the kids. He had stopped camping out at Will Geer's and Leadbelly's apartments and rented several rooms on 101st Street. In a letter to Mary Jo he said he'd bought a new Chevrolet, but almost as if a warning bell were sounding about catering to a wealthier lifestyle, he added, "For God's sake, don't be . . . afraid to think what you want to and say what you please."

One of Woody's favorite phrases was "Hold the phone!"— meaning "Stop!" or "Wait!" If he had said those words to himself before the year 1940 drew to an end, he might have been prepared for what down-homers in Oklahoma called "the chickens coming home to roost." Directors of the CBS and NBC radio shows began to ask Woody to think more about pleasing audiences and sponsors. They advised him not to say certain words, not to bring up certain topics. They wanted him to wear makeup, or dress like a clown, or prance onto the stage. They decided his "Woody Sez" column, carried now by the communist newspaper *The Daily Worker*, was not acceptable.

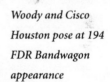

Woody and Cisco Houston pose at 194 FDR Bandwagon appearance

When he did actually stop writing the column, he felt it was his first real sell out. Immediately, old angers rushed in at him. Guilt turned sideways into stubbornness. "Hold the phone!" he finally told himself. No way would he be a fat cat in the big city, all

Alan Lomax playing guitar on stage at Mountain Music Festival, Asheville, North Carolina, 1935

starched up and wrinkle free. He'd rather hop the freights with drifters like himself than ride first class on any New York Money Express. Though Mary had felt secure, carrying three hundred dollars in her purse while he was on big-time radio, she just might have to repack their suitcases.

Woody had interviewed for a singing job at the swank Rainbow Room in Rockefeller Center, where red roses "as wide as your hand" floated in water-filled glass bowls on each table. Called back for a second interview, he tried out a few humorous verses he'd made up. "This Rainbow Room," he began, "she's mighty fine. You can spit from here to th' Texas line!" When he finished, he heard the manager and his assistant discussing costumes for him.

"French peasant garb!" suggested the assistant.

"No!" the manager answered. "I see him as a Louisiana swamp dweller, half asleep on the flat top of a gum stump, his feet dangling in the mud, and his gun leaning near his head!"

"Imagine!" replied the assistant. "What the proper costuming will bring out in these people! Their carefree life! Open skies! The quaint simplicity!"

Hold the phone! Woody paced back and forth, peering out the windows of the Rainbow Room toward the street sixty-five stories below him. Crushed pieces of newspaper floated over the trash bins and awnings. They seemed to be waving at him. When the assistant smugly talked to him about the customers always being right, he picked up his guitar and asked directions to the Men's Room. Out in the hallway, however, he spied an elevator sign, and a few minutes later he was strolling across the marble floors of the lobby. Plucking his guitar, he began singing country and blues tunes at the top of his lungs.

Passersby stopped in their tracks. A poodle on a leash by the front desk laid back its ears. Woody would write that people had been walking "hushed up and too nice and quiet through these tiled floors too long," that he wanted them to see someone "not singing because he was hired and told what to sing, but just walking through there thinking about the world and singing about it."

He sidestepped a scowling, red-faced policeman, pushed through the revolving doors, and was out on the crowded winter street. He jogged for hours alongside the clanging, clattering traffic, occasionally strumming notes on his guitar. At dusk he glanced up at the maze of tall office buildings. They didn't look anything like the paint-chipped barns of southwestern prairies. His own father and mother had welcomed the country life. They hadn't been swallowed up by the city. Not everyone believed in the "stock market tickers . . . plugged in like juke boxes [*sic*], playing the false and corny lies that are sung in the wild canyons of Wall Street."

Woody Guthrie (left) and Burl Ives in promo pose in New York's Central Park

Woody took a deep breath of fresh air. Heading toward 101st Street, he was glad to have cut loose from CBS and NBC and the glass bowls in Rockefeller Center. He had a storm of words and music inside him, a high gospel fire—but not a bit of sissified hogwash. Always, he would want his songs to be honest—to have "fight and guts and belly laughs and power."

chapter SIX

I worked in your orchard of peaches and prunes,
Slept on the ground in the light of your moon,
On the edge of your city you've seen us and then,
We come with the dust and we go with the wind.

California and Arizona, I make all your crops,
And it's north up to Oregon to gather your hops,
Dig the beets from your ground, cut the grapes from your vines,
To set on your table your light sparkling wine.

Green pastures of plenty from dry desert ground,
From that Grand Coulee Dam where the water runs down,
Every state in this union us migrants have been,
We work in this fight, and we'll fight till we win.

Well, it's always we ramble, that river and I,
All along your green valleys I'll work till I die,
My land I'll defend with my life, if it be,
'Cause my pastures of plenty must always be free.

—"PASTURES OF PLENTY"

Migrants traveling east of Oklahoma, 1939

oody blew out of New York without a "So long." With Mary, Teeny, Sue, and little Will Rogers (called Bill) piled in the car, along with suitcases, snacks, and toys he'd made for the kids out of wooden blocks, he drove through a storm to Alan Lomax's house in Washington, D.C. The family stayed the night, then careened south into Louisiana to visit Woody's half uncle Lawrence Tanner, who'd heard Woody turned Communist and shooed them away. From there they visited Matt Jennings's home in El Paso, Texas. Matt seemed shocked that Woody was no longer with the "big bucks" in New York, but Mary—looking weary—simply shook her head.

In Columbia, California, a ghost town that had

once been a gold rush boomtown, Woody rented one large hotel room. For two weeks he pounded away on an old typewriter he bought from Matt for ten dollars. Though he and Mary argued, he didn't mind the kids being underfoot. He began his autobiography—Alan Lomax's idea—and wrote letters to Leadbelly, Cisco Houston, and Pete Seeger. Pete had formed a folksinging group with Lee Hays, a songwriter from Arkansas, and Millard Lampell, a writer from New Jersey. They'd named themselves the Almanac Singers. The United States would soon become involved in World War II, which was already devasting Europe, and the Almanacs composed and performed peace songs.

Woody had a lot to say about the war. He hated both Adolph Hitler, who'd been bragging about his murderous Nazi Party, and Benito Mussolini, head of the Fascists in Italy, who touted the oppression of the individual by the state. "The enemy is out there in plain sight," Woody said.

From Columbia the family went to Los Angeles where hungry Okies, replaced by hungrier Mexicans, had vacated the migrant camps to work in war munitions factories. Woody thought he'd be back on KFVD, but Frank Burke—still angry over the arguments they'd had—wouldn't hire him. Nor would landlords rent to him, not when they saw the children. After sleeping nights in the car, the family finally ended up, dirty and disheveled, in leftist writer Ed Robbin's yard. Next door, Ed said, was a vacant cottage that they just might be able to rent from its stubborn eighty-year-old owner. Woody drove to Mrs. Wolfson's apartment in Pasadena, serenaded her for an hour, and charmed her into agreeing to a ten-dollar monthly rent for her cottage. Mrs. Wolfson, however, never asked him to pay up.

At the cottage Woody typed out his thoughts and continued working on his life story. Ed Robbin would write that the typewriter was "going like a riveting machine, all hours of the day and night. . . .

I don't know when he slept." Of course, no money was coming in—no sign painting, cartooning, or dishwashing jobs, not even guitar playing in saloons for a capful of coins. Woody pawned a radio to feed the family, joking that his next song would be called "Hock-shop Rag"—but then a registered letter arrived from Oregon. The Bonneville Power Administration (BPA) in Portland wanted him to write songs for a film to help raise operating funds for two new dams on the Columbia River.

The Grand Coulee and Bonneville Dams were a government effort to bring low-cost electricity to rural homes and under-developed areas in Oregon, a project opposed by private power companies. To Woody, the dams were a way to harness water power for the common good, while also providing work for the jobless and electricity to needy households. Once again the battered suit-cases were packed. In the car the Guthrie kids tumbled over the stained upholstery, peering out through a cracked window to say good-bye to Ed and his wife.

In Portland, Woody learned that the proposed film didn't yet have solid backing, but the administrator of the BPA had gotten him a special thirty-day position for $266.66. Thus began the most prolific work period of his life. The BPA sent him "to read books about the Coulee and Bonneville dams, to walk around up and down the river, and to see what I could find to make up songs about."

Awed by the grandeur of the Pacific Northwest, he talked to dozens of lumberjacks, bulldozer drivers, construction workers, jackhammer men, welders, and concrete pourers. He drank with the men in bars, listening to them talk while he gulped down hot chili (his favorite food). He was, he told them, "nothin' but a little rusty-voiced guitar picker"—but some of them knew his reputation. *Wasn't he that guy who sang about a fair shake for everybody?*

Hunched over his typewriter or scribbling in notebooks, Woody wrote twenty-six songs in about the same number of days. Haunting, lyrical, poetic, and sometimes funny, the songs would become a permanent part of folk Americana. Their range of style and tempo was astounding. Sung by him through loudspeakers in the BPA offices, they expressed all the pride of the power project and were soon on everyone's lips.

Known as the *Columbia River Collection,* the songs included ballads (light, simple songs), work songs (songs sung to accompany tasks or labors), talking blues (songs of melancholy, originating among black Americans), and anthems (songs of praise, devotion, or patriotism). Woody often used tunes from existing songs that weren't his own, a common practice among folk writers, making them easy for listeners to remember. The tune to Leadbelly's "Goodnight Irene" became the tune to Woody's "Roll On, Columbia" (designated in 1987 as the official Washington State folk song). The tune to the ballad "Pretty Polly" became Woody's "Pastures of Plenty," which he wrote after visiting government-funded migrant camps outside Portland that actually had tents, running water, and medical care.

In addition to the tunes he borrowed, he created many of his own melodies. Some of the Columbia River songs were majestic and melodramatic:

THE GRAND COULEE DAM
She winds down the granite canyon, and she bends across the lea,
Like a prancing dancing stallion down her seaway to the sea;
Cast your eyes upon the biggest thing yet built by human
    hands,
On the King Columbia River, it's the big Grand Coulee Dam.
In the misty crystal glitter of the wild and windward spray,
Men have fought the pounding waters, and met a watr'y grave,

Well she tore their boats to splinters and she gave men
  dreams to dream,
Of the day the Coulee Dam would cross that wild and wasted
  stream.

ROLL ON, COLUMBIA

Green Douglas firs where the waters cut through,
Down her wild mountains and canyons she flew.
Canadian Northwest to the ocean so blue,
Roll on, Columbia, roll on!
  [Refrain]
Roll on, Columbia, roll on,
Roll on, Columbia, roll on.
Your power is turning our darkness to dawn,
So, roll on, Columbia, roll on!

Some of the songs suggested the pulsing beat of the machines
used to build the Grand Coulee and Bonneville Dams:

JACKHAMMER JOHN

I'm a jackhammer man from a jackhammer town,
I can hammer on a hammer till the sun goes down.
I hammered on the Boulder, hammered on the Butte,
Columbia River on the Five Mile Schute.

And some of the songs were ironic and humorous:

IT TAKES A MARRIED MAN TO SING A WORRIED SONG

Well you single boys can ramble,
  you single boys can roam,
But it takes a married man, boys,
  to sing a worried song.

55

THE TALKIN' BLUES

Now if you want to get to heaven let me tell you what to do
Just grease your feet with a little mutton stew,
And slide out of the devil's hand,
Just ooze over into the promised land.
But take it easy—go greasy.

When Woody's month at the dams ended, he had made such an impression on power station officials that one day in the future a building at the BPA would be named for him. But he wasn't sure, in that early summer of 1941, where he'd go next or what he'd do—until Pete Seeger invited him to join the Almanac Singers on a driving spree across the country, singing out for unions and strikers. *Yippee!* Mary and the children, he decided, could wait for him in Portland while he was away.

The morning that the letter came from Pete, a snooty, tie-wearing man turned up on the doorstep of the motel where the Guthries were staying. Woody, it turned out, had made only one payment on his car, and the finance company man had tracked him down through several states to repossess it. Woody didn't say much, just slung his guitar over his shoulder. A car was just a car, wasn't it? Just a convenience that cost money? Not something owned by the families that had trudged down Route 66 out of the Dust Bowl. Mary and the kids would be okay; they liked riding the buses.

Besides, Woody assured himself, how could anyone compare the value of a car with a Pacific Northwest sunset over the rolling Columbia River, with the reach of the Douglas fir trees into the sky—or, come to think of it, even with a pot of steaming-hot chili?

❰ ❰ ❰

The driving trip was as zany a time as that long tramp through the desert hunting for Jerry P. Guthrie's silver mine. The Almanacs' tour, organized at CIO union headquarters in New York, began on July 4, 1941, in Philadelphia and ended in September in San Francisco. With Woody (now twenty-nine years old) driving their rusted 1929 Buick, with Pete, Lee Hays, and Millard Lampell spread out over the seats, the troupe juggled a kaleidoscope of cities. The Almanacs laughed, talked, ate, argued, told silly jokes, spit, slept, drank whiskey, and made up dozens of songs. Purposely dressed in faded shirts and old pants to separate themselves from highfalutin' rich folks, they spilled into union halls and onto picket lines. More than two million workers in America were on strike, the highest number since 1919.

The Almanacs, Woody would say, "sang before, during, and after the [union] speakers had spoke [*sic*], and took up a collection

The Almanac Singers (left to right): Woody Guthrie, Millard Lampell, Bess Lomax, Pete Seeger, Arthur Stern, Sis Cunningham, circa 1941

to buy gas, oil, and to grease the breezes. We sang 'Union Maid,' 'Talking Union,' 'I Don't Want Your Millions Mister,' 'Get Thee Behind Me Satan,' 'Union Train a' Comin'. . . . [We] sang for five thousand longshoremen at the Harry Bridges local. We sang for the Ladies Auxiliary. We sang for the farm and factory workers." In Cleveland they appeared at the National Maritime Union convention; in Illinois they joined the striking furriers in Cicero. "Our good music," Woody said, "actually tamed down this gang of thugs and kept a big fight from breaking out."

On a Minneapolis picket line at the International Harvester plant, the Almanacs were caught in a tear-gas attack set off by the National Guard. But to their delight, they saw that their songs were helping promote union membership, that more and more companies were surrendering to the idea of workers being organized by the unions. Woody's songs, and those written by the Almanacs, clearly expressed working-class struggles and would make popular the term *protest song*. They were, Woody said, "right out of the workers' lives."

When the Almanacs were in Los Angeles, Mary brought the children (five, three, and almost two years old) from Portland, Oregon, to Pampa, Texas, and telephoned Woody. With a new firmness and finality to her voice, she finally confronted him about the future. He'd stay with the Almanacs, he told her, and give New York another try. He could move the family with him, but he'd still be going on the road. No, Mary said. No more. She, Teeny, Sue, and Bill were returning to Texas. She would file for divorce.

Woody remembered how young they'd been when they married. They hadn't really known each other, hadn't really known themselves. He'd admit to having shirked his responsibilities, but of their relationship he'd say only, "She was right from her side and I was right from my side."

In New York the Almanacs could look forward to six or seven bookings a week. They shared an apartment, where Woody stashed all his writings in a steamer trunk, and where Sundays were given over to songfests called hootenannies (as Woody and Pete had heard them referred to on tour). Singers and guests who paid thirty-five cents' admission, were a fascinating, if shaggy, crew, and included such regulars as blind harmonica player Sonny Terry and folk artist Bess Lomax (Alan's sister), plus intellectuals, poets, writers, neighborhood drunks, young female groupies, and Communist activists.

Their bookings generally went from 7 P.M. to 2 A.M. Rambling onto subway trains with their guitars, banjos, and mandolins, the Almanacs might astonish passengers by performing for them right there in the aisles. They were even booked at some fancy parties, where Woody sometimes walked out if he got fed up with the snobbishness, or disrupted the goings-on by lambasting "high rents, robbing landlords, fake real estate racketeers, loan sharks . . . and punk politicians."

He sang with the Almanacs until 1943, when they all went their separate ways. By then, American soldiers had begun fighting in World War II, and the Almanacs switched from peace songs to morale-boosting war songs, becoming the first organized singing group to broadcast anti-Hitler tunes on the radio.

Woody's songs for his next job, however, were a far cry from his war songs. A New York dancer, Sophie Maslow, had choreographed dances to some of his Dust Bowl ballads and asked him to sing as the dances were performed. Rehearsals took place in a chilly studio on Thirteenth Street run by the renowned teacher and dancer Martha Graham. Woody found it almost impossible, however, to keep practicing his verses in exactly the same rhythm. He would pause at whim, interrupting the flow of the dancers' movements.

Frustrated, Sophie was about to replace him when another dancer, Marjorie Mazia, intervened.

Small, delicate, and beautiful, Marjorie glided across the floor toward Woody. She told him that his ballad "Tom Joad" was her favorite song. She told him to get some shirt cardboards from a cleaner, and that she would mark on them the precise counting for each word and pause in his ballads. He could keep the cardboards in front of him while he sang. "Now, Woody," she said, "if you can count, you can do this."

As she spoke, Marjorie seemed to be looking right through him, past the wiry, slightly defiant tilt of his head, beyond the wary glint in his eyes. The cardboard guides helped enormously. During rehearsal breaks Woody watched Marjorie's every move. After the other dancers had wearily shrugged on their coats to go home at night, he sat with her on the studio floor, talking quietly, his usual jokes forgotten. She was married, she said, but lived apart from her husband. Woody remembered meeting many women on the road who had wanted him to stay the night with them, and marriage to Mary hadn't stopped him from agreeing. But Marjorie, whose tenderness seemed to him as soothing as one of his mother's lullabies from his childhood, made him suddenly shy.

He walked her home on those winter nights, making certain she was safe. They sometimes stopped at a sidewalk café for coffee and rolls, warming themselves over the cups. One snowy night in February, as they strolled down the street and Marjorie chatted about her Russian-Jewish immigrant parents and how she'd taught dance at a left-wing summer camp, Woody worked up the courage to take her hand.

As they neared the brownstone boardinghouse on Fourteenth Street where Marjorie lived, they paused. A small rip in Marjorie's glove had brought Woody to a halt. Beneath the torn edges of yarn he could feel the bare skin of her slender finger. It was as if he had never touched anyone before.

In shock, Woody stared at Marjorie Mazia. Her dark hair glistened under the street lamp, and flakes of snow twinkled on her coat. He found it utterly amazing in that moment that the warmth of Marjorie's finger could feel better than any song.

chapter SEVEN

Love casts out hate.
Love gets rid of all fears.
Love washes all clean.
Love forgives all debts.
Love forgets all mistakes.
Love overcomes all errors and excuses
  and pardons and understands the key
  reasons why the mistake, the error,
  the stumble, the sprawl, the fall, was made.
Love heals all.
  —"BORN TO WIN"

Book-jacket portrait of
Woody for Bound for Glory

Woody was still drawn to the seamy side of New York City, performing in greasy saloons, spending nights in flophouses along Third Avenue or in the Bowery. He told Marjorie he'd been "pushed off the main road" early in life, and part of him was still the "rebellious kid." Twenty-five-year-old Marjorie was an organizing center for him. She accepted, even admired, his headstrong nature, but she also reminded him to bathe or brush his teeth. She let him use her apartment when she traveled with Martha Graham, and insisted he work every day on his autobiography as if it were a regular job.

Woody wrote letters to her, each dozens of pages

in length. Under his hillbilly swagger, he wrote, he had felt "like [he] was drowning in an ocean full of burning oil and [she] pulled [him] out." When she told him she was pregnant and the child was due in the winter of 1943, he was thrilled. They'd both be divorced by then, he said, and they'd get married. A baby was a sign they belonged together.

Woody loved Teeny, Sue, and Bill, but this anticipated child with Marjorie seemed miraculous to him. He sent money to Mary in his haphazard way, stuffing the envelopes with cartoons and comments. He'd been thinking, he told her, of enlisting in the army or navy, since America needed all the war help it could get to defeat the Nazis and Fascists, but until then he hoped his songs might promote justice and humanity in the world. "Music," he said, "is a weapon, the same as a gun."

During and after World War II, Woody, Pete Seeger, Lee Hays, Leadbelly, Bess Lomax, and ten other folk artists kept the "weapon" of their music alive. In 1946, they would form a new group, People's Songs. Lyrics would be provided for union meetings, parties, and fund-raisers, and advice dispensed on creating songbooks, applying for copyrights, and marketing songs. Woody chose song subjects from newspaper articles on "wrecks, accidents, fires, floods, droughts, hurricanes, cyclones, . . . family squabbles, lovers' troubles, . . . gangster fights, bad houses, slum diseases." And he wrote often about politics, greed, racial intolerance, and war.

Soon after the U.S. battleship *Reuben James*, carrying a large crew, was destroyed in World War II by enemy fire, Woody was at his typewriter:

THE SINKING OF THE *REUBEN JAMES*

Have you heard of a ship called the good *Reuben James*,
Manned by hard fighting men both of honor and fame?

She flew the stars and stripes of this land of the free,
Tonight she's in her grave on the bottom of the sea.

Tell me, what were their names, tell me, what were their
    names?
Did you have a friend on the good *Reuben James*?
What were their names, tell me what were their names,
Did you have a friend on the good *Reuben James*?

Woody encouraged everyone, young and old, to write honest stories into songs. "You can write it down," he said, "with the stub of a burnt match, or with an old chewed up penny pencil, on the back of a sack . . . or you could pitch in and write your walls full of your own songs."

As he wrote down his autobiography, Alan and Bess Lomax took the chapters to an editor at E. P. Dutton publishers. In the rambling, raw paragraphs the editor found the gold of an authentic writer. Woody's tale of his Oklahoma childhood and later years burst from the pages. Although the unfinished manuscript would need heavy editing, E. P. Dutton offered Woody a contract: $500 in advance. He jumped at the offer and arranged for Mary to receive twenty-five dollars a week, for at least six months.

He divided writing time between his book, which he called *Boomchasers,* and a journal he'd begun for his future baby—whom he nicknamed "Railroad Pete." He was alarmed when Marjorie suddenly decided to return to her husband Arnold's home in Delaware until the baby was born. She knew Arnold would arrange for fine medical care, and she promised Woody she'd be back by spring. She'd ask Arnold for a divorce and tell her parents that she planned to marry a non-Jew.

Anxious, Woody turned to his Railroad Pete journal, pouring his feelings out as if he were confiding in a trusted friend:

I am stormy like the weather and I do a lot of useless tossing and whirling and pitching but [Marjorie] is as well organized as the sky and everything goes to its place. . . .

. . . girl or boy, you will be loved an equal amount. And if you are twins or quintuplets or something like that, then there will just be that many more to lick fascism. A girl can do just as much in any field as a boy, to beat fascism—although I'm hoping this is one monster that your eye won't have to see—; yet you may—because the world is full of hesitators and long waiters.

One sentence in Woody's journal expressed a gnawing fear he may have harbored ever since learning that his mother died from Huntington's chorea: "I have dreams that tell me I'm not entirely as sane as is comfortable."

With Marjorie in Delaware, Woody spent his time filling more notebooks "talking" to Railroad Pete and performing at union halls with Sonny Terry and Leadbelly. He'd rented a tiny, fourth-floor walk-up on Charles Street in Manhattan for twenty-seven dollars a month, and with his own book finished, he lugged into the apartment library books by writers that caught his fancy—Walt Whitman, Aleksandr Pushkin, Carl Sandburg, Maxim Gorky. He'd written a war song, "Talking Hitler's Head Off Blues," that was printed in the *Daily Worker* newspaper. In a fit of patriotism and faith in the impact of song, he painted on his guitar THIS MACHINE KILLS FASCISTS.

On February 6, 1943, Cathy Ann Guthrie was born. With a silent salute to Railroad Pete, Woody began a new journal entry. "Howdy little Miss Cathy Ann," he wrote. He hitched a ride to visit Marjorie and Cathy at the hospital in Delaware and stood for an hour in front of the nursery window, spellbound by his tiny child. He could barely tear himself away to return to New

*Woody and
his painted guitar*

York. Only Marjorie's vow that she would join him by April gave him peace.

In March, E. P. Dutton published Woody's autobiography, having renamed it *Bound for Glory* after Woody's song "This Train Is Bound for Glory." Woody sent off the first autographed copy to his

67

father in Oklahoma City and hoped readers would realize that it was the worker, not himself, who was bound for glory. Most readers were captivated by his story. Though some reviews mentioned the tediousness of the Okie dialogue or said the events were too contrived, others were filled with praise. "A huge, rich, juicy chunk of life," said *Book Week*. "Woody is on fire inside, a natural born poet," said the *New York Times Book Review*. "Some day people are going to wake up to the fact," the *New Yorker* prophesied, "that Woody Guthrie and the ten thousand songs that leap and tumble off the strings of his music box are a national possession, like Yellowstone or Yosemite."

Woody was a celebrity again in New York City. He was asked to be on radio shows and was invited to posh parties. E. P. Dutton offered him a contract for another book and assigned him a public relations adviser. For a while, he was followed around by a *Life* magazine photographer. On April 15, in a borrowed car, he brought Marjorie and Cathy from Delaware to his apartment on Charles Street, and agreed that Marjorie could look for larger quarters.

But soon, just as during his first New York experience—and even with Marjorie and Cathy to soothe him—he felt trapped by his success. When Cisco Houston needled him about talking a good war game but not living it, Woody went down to the Maritime Union Hall and signed up with the merchant marines. He, Cisco, and a friend named Jimmy Longhi were assigned to mess, or kitchen, duty on the ship *William B. Travis*, which carried war supplies across the Atlantic.

Marjorie reluctantly supported his enlistment. She had found a temporary apartment near her parents, a short walk from the Coney Island beach, and she and Cathy would wait there for him. She was aware of the contrast between thirty-one-year-old Woody, small-framed and short, and the tall, muscled, battle-trained sailors on the *Travis*. When Woody went aboard with his guitar, a mandolin, harmonicas, a Jew's harp, a typewriter, books, and notebooks, she thought he'd be eaten alive by the other men, but as it turned out, he became a kind of witty, exuberant mascot for them.

Woody sailed on three major assignments for the merchant marine. The huge supply ships (often carrying two-ton bombs and gasoline) were guarded by destroyer ships that sent down depth charges to destroy enemy torpedoes and submarines. Woody built the sailors a wind machine from wood, pulleys, gears, small propellers, and rubberbands that became the talk of the ship. On deck and in the mess hall he'd strum his guitar and belt out union songs or patriotic war songs. Hard-bitten and tough as the men were, they'd briefly put a halt to their duties to sing along, shouting or bellowing the words, their eyes often misting over.

"It seems," Woody said of the men, "like you get to thinking about everything both good and bad that you've done in your whole life, and you sort of let it all gather up inside your system, and you see that you are out there risking your life, and you just want to lay your head back and wiggle your ears and sing so loud and so long that all of the good and the bad will sort of mix up and boil around and come out of you. You feel that way. Every man does."

A month later, the *Travis* was torpedoed off the coast of Sicily, with one man killed and dozens hurt. Woody had now experienced the harsh reality of war. The crew was transported to the nearest harbor by lifeboats while the ship slowly sank. As he awaited orders in the city of Palermo, Woody played poker with Cisco and Jimmy, and sent daily letters to Marjorie and Cathy. Finally he was reassigned to several short crossings and took mess duty on the *William Floyd*. Its cargo included two hundred oil-field workers headed for North Africa. At Arzew, as the ship unloaded, he was overwhelmed by the sight of starving Algerians in rags begging for food, moaning and clawing their way to the ship. He gave them his next several meals, collected other food and bags of soap for them, and two days later, in the center of town, serenaded their skin-and-bones children.

On Woody's last assignment, aboard the *Sea Porpoise* in 1944, the "supplies" were three thousand soldiers headed for active duty in France, hoping to help end World War II. One night in mid-June, while gunfire flamed and hissed across the skies and torpedoes grazed the *Sea Porpoise,* Woody heard depth charges sounding like graveyard thunder. Jumping from his berth, suddenly overwhelmed by memories of Okemah's cyclone when he was six, he grabbed his guitar and rounded up Cisco and Jimmy. "Let's go!" he yelled, indicating the five mammoth holds at the bottom of the ship that contained the three thousand soldiers. When his two friends looked at him like he was crazy, he ran off alone. The soldiers, he'd decided, needed a distraction. If the *Sea Porpoise* was torpedoed, no men would make it out of the holds. If he went down with them, so be it.

For two hours Woody ran from hold to hold, playing his guitar, shouting out happy songs, leading square-dance routines for the soldiers. Sweat and laughter filled the air. No outsider viewing the scene would have guessed the ship was on the verge of catastrophe. As it happened, the *Sea Porpoise* survived that night on the Atlantic only to be crippled near Normandy by an acoustic mine, activated by sound, that exploded beneath it. Fortunately, everyone escaped.

Whenever Woody looked back on his stint in the merchant marine, he heard in his mind the heartfelt singing of the three thousand soldiers in their cavernous holds, joining together to defy the menace of German submarines. Even though he had come smack up against a danger far different from the perils of his childhood, he had met it head-on. After all, he would say, the *William B. Travis,* the *William Floyd,* and the *Sea Porpoise*— proud ships of World War II—had given him "a full cargo of memories."

chapter **EIGHT**

Well, what brings me here, I guess you are asking.
I know folks did watch down this road I have come,
I've come several trips on bright nights of moonlight,
And other nights come in the winds and the storms.

The ground it doth moan and the earth it's a-trembling;
Our trees and our flowers, they dance in the wind;
The flowers they whine and the wild wind is whistling
As I kiss this ground down on the mound of your grave.

—"THE MOUND OF YOUR GRAVE"

Woody's cartoon about solving problems

On the day Germany surrendered to the Allies—May 7, 1945—Woody was drafted into the army. The standard deferment from army service because of having children to support had ended. The timing for Woody was so bizarre that, reading his induction orders, he said of Hitler, "He must have seen me coming in!" Over the next eight months he was stationed in New Jersey, Texas, Illinois, and Nevada, where he earned a teletype degree. His too-big uniform swam on him, and army life seemed lonelier than being in the merchant marine, but he made the best of it. Mary brought Teeny, Sue, and Bill to see him in Texas, and Marjorie visited in Illinois.

Woody had a two-week furlough in November

before reporting to the Nevada base. He hitched rides into New York City, and since both their divorces had finally been issued, he and Marjorie got married at City Hall. He hoped he could be a good husband to her. "I would quit anything," he told her, "to build up my days around yours."

When he was discharged, he joined Marjorie and Cathy on Coney Island in a tiny, three-room apartment at 3520 Mermaid Avenue. Fewer than ten miles from Manhattan, Coney Island jutted out into the paper-littered water, its boardwalk lined with amusement park rides and hot-dog stands. Woody was happy with his little family and chronicled all of Cathy's activities in journals—toys she played with, rhymes she learned, questions she asked. Dark-haired like Woody, she had an exuberance that glowed in her face.

Pete Seeger, too, had married, and Woody met up with him again at the New York home of Seeger's in-laws. "[He] saw my guitar," Woody said, "unslung his banjo, and before we could shake hands or pass many blessings, we had played, 'Sally Goodin,' 'Doggy Spit a Rye Straw,' 'Going Down This Road Feeling Bad,' 'Worried Man Blues,' and 'Fifteen Miles from Birmingham.'" People's Songs had formed a branch division, People's Artists, which booked singers and speakers for left-wing rallies. Soon Woody appeared at postwar events with Pete, Leadbelly, Cisco Houston, and singers Earl Robinson and Burl Ives.

Woody met a man named Moses (Moe) Asch, who loved American folk music and owned a pint-size record company on West Forty-sixth Street. Woody dropped in unannounced and sat on the floor while Asch peered down at him from a desk chair. "I want to make some records," Woody said. "So," countered the heavyset Asch, "when do you want to start?"

With a beer or two under his belt, an unshaven Woody came evenings to the studio and stood before a microphone in a closet-like room, strumming his guitar and singing his heart out. Sometimes he brought Sonny Terry and Cisco Houston to record with him. Asch, he said, "took us in, cranked up his machinery and told us to fire away with everything that we had. We yelled and whooped and beat and pounded till Asch had taken down One Hundred and Twenty Some Odd Master [*sic*] sides."

One of Woody's recordings, "This Land Is Your Land," would become his most famous song. He'd created it in answer to Irving Berlin's "God Bless America," a popular anthem that annoyed him because it made America seem too sticky sweet. Moe Asch said that he knew at once the song was special:

THIS LAND IS YOUR LAND

[Chorus]
This land is your land, this land is my land,
From California to the New York island;
From the redwood forest to the Gulf Stream waters,
This land was made for you and me.

As I was walking that ribbon of highway,
I saw above me that endless skyway;
I saw below me that golden valley;
This land was made for you and me.

. . . .

On a bright and sunny morning,
In the shadow of the steeple,
By the relief office I seen my people;
As they stood there hungry, I stood there wondering,
Is this land made for you and me?

. . . .

[Chorus]
Nobody living can ever stop me,
As I go walking that freedom highway;

Nobody living can ever make me turn back;
This land was made for you and me.

On subway rides between Coney Island and Asch Record Company, Woody began hearing a surge of anti-Communist talk. A postwar alliance between Russia and the U.S. unraveled, and Joseph Stalin, the Soviet Union's leader, was hurling criticisms at America. The animosity between the two countries would soon be referred to as the Cold War. Woody was still grateful for the support given by Communists to the plight of American workers. "Everything," he

Cathy Ann Guthrie

insisted, "is a part of the conflict between the boss man and the work hand." He believed in any political system that closed the gap between rich and poor and would never "make hoboes nor bums nor dirty backdoor tramps out of any of us."

Telling this story in song became the thrust of New York hootenannies in 1946. Woody saw his messages inspiring workers "to band together and to talk, think, plan, and fight together." Authentic folk music, performed with pride by the artists of People's Songs, had been making inroads in urban cities beyond New York, such as Chicago and San Francisco; its artists were now hired to perform in nightclubs and hotels.

In the apartment on Coney Island, Woody was writing up a storm. He sent letters to politicians, labor leaders, and people in the news. He mailed off notes to his brothers Roy and George, sister Mary Jo, and his father. He wrote a column in the left-wing *Sunday Worker* newspaper and jotted down his thoughts—which he called "Coney Island Short Hauls"—in notebooks. A pencil usually stuck out of his back pocket or protruded from behind one ear.

What he wasn't writing, however, was his second book (which he'd named *Ship Story*) for E. P. Dutton. He'd produce three or four pages, then crumple them up. His thoughts seemed to spin out of his head, and he had trouble concentrating. Maybe it was the fault of his daily beer or wine, he told himself.

He was most relaxed when he and Marjorie took Cathy, perched piggyback on his shoulders, to the beach or the shops. He'd beam as Cathy greeted passersby in her lilting voice, and he wrote down her conversations. "Daddy," she'd say, "why doesn't Mr. Sun Shine shine [*sic*] all the time?" or "Mommy, will my teacher bring Mister Sun Shine into my school room?"

Woody and Marjorie in a publicity shot for their children's hootenannies

When Marjorie was dancing in New York City, Woody babysat for Cathy while trying, without success, to begin his book. Instead of writing, he and Cathy played marbles or made music by beating with spoons on tin cans, oatmeal boxes, or tambourines. He composed children's songs for his daughter, flabbergasted at how she memorized and sang them over and over to herself:

WHY, OH WHY

Why can't a bird eat an elephant?
Why, oh why, oh why?
'Cause an elephant's got a pretty hard skin.
Goodbye, goodbye, goodbye.

MAIL MYSELF TO YOU

I'm a-gonna wrap myself in paper,
I'm gonna daub myself with glue,
Stick some stamps on top of my head;
I'm gonna mail myself to you.

I'm a-gonna tie me up in a red string,
I'm gonna tie blue ribbons too,
I'm a-gonna climb up in my mailbox;
I'm gonna mail myself to you.
When you see me in your mailbox,
Cut the string and let me out;
Wash the glue off my fingers,
Stick some bubble-gum in my mouth.

Take me out of my wrapping paper,
Wash the stamps off my head;
Pour me full of ice cream sodies,
Put me in my nice warm bed.

Woody's children's songs weren't written "down" to their young audience; they spoke to children's curiosity and humor. Though some of Woody's friends criticized him for spending time on such "simple" creations, Moe Asch understood Woody's wanting to build a bridge into a child's world. With Marjorie at his side, Woody recorded dozens of children's songs at Asch Records. Distributed in albums along with small pamphlets of lyrics, photos of Cathy, and Woody's drawings of children, they gradually became staples in homes and nursery schools across the country.

In the pamphlet for *Work Songs to Grow On* was Woody's philosophy:

Let your kids teach you how to act these songs out, these and a thousand other songs. Get the whole fam damily [*sic*] into the fun. Get papa, mama, brother, sister, aunt, uncle, grandma, grandpa, all your neighbors, friends, visitors, and everybody else in on it. . . .

Watch the kids. Do like they do. Act like they act. Yell like they yell. Dance like they dance. Sing like they sing. Work like the kids do. You'll be plenty healthy, and feel pretty wealthy, and live to be wise, if you put these songs or any earthly song, on your radio, record player, or on your lips, and do like the kids do. I don't want the kids to be grown up, I want to see the grownups be kids.

The year 1946 had been one of big strikes and long picket lines. During the war, unions were wary of demanding benefits for workers when young men were dying on the battlefields by the hundreds of thousands. But now that peace had come, unions were back in gear. After the United Electrical Workers called a strike at Pittsburgh's Westinghouse Electric Company, Woody, Pete Seeger, and Lee Hays flew in from New York.

Twenty thousand workers and their families marched angrily down the streets, waving flags and banners, the largest gathering of its kind in Pittsburgh's history. Policemen circled the crowds on motorcycles. Woody was recognized by many of the strikers, who told him over and over that his songs had changed lives. "You're like one of the Bible prophets," one striker said. "Centuries ago, they sang the important news—and so do you!" "You give us *truth* songs," exclaimed another man, "not music for fooling ourselves!"

As strikes erupted across the country Woody noticed a profound change among unions. No longer did organizers meet secretly around campfires. No longer were conflicts settled by a punch in the jaw. Unions, representing most major industries, had become an American fixture. Run by tough administrators and financial experts, they negotiated not only for higher wages, but for eight-hour workdays, overtime pay, health insurance, and retirement plans. And union leaders had developed increasing clout nationally, sometimes ignoring the feelings of their membership. To Woody's shock, the National Maritime Union, one of his favorites, gave in to the country's anti-Communist fever and fired some of their loyal but pro-Communist officials.

People's Songs were also affected by anti-Communist sentiment and found themselves hired for fewer gigs. The term left wing, which applied to the socialist/communist leanings of both People's Songs and People's Artists, was now a slur. Still, fans at hootenannies sometimes numbered over three hundred. At a hootenanny in the Newspaper Guild Hall, Woody put three-year-old Cathy onstage, where she sang some of his children's songs. Cheeks red with excitement, she ran up and down the aisles and sat in the laps of people who beckoned to her.

Flint, Michigan, National Guardsmen draw guns at a strike, 1937

The Guthrie apartment had become a haven for troubled teenagers in the neighborhood who liked the freewheeling lifestyle there. While Cathy served them cookies, they confided their problems to Marjorie, listened raptly to Woody's message songs and, even though there was so little space, often camped out on a cot or the floor.

On February 6, 1947, Cathy turned four years old. Her birthday drawings were lovingly saved by her "Pa." Four days later Woody left for Elizabeth, New Jersey, to perform for the union of Phelps-Dodge electrical workers as they celebrated the end of an eight-month strike. By late afternoon he'd gone into New York City to discuss records with Moe Asch, who'd found enough money to put out six more Woody songs on three records. *Billboard,* a respected music publication, applauded the songs for their "social significance" and appeal to "the man on the back street."

Returning to his apartment on Mermaid Avenue, Woody smelled smoke in the first-floor hallway. Taped onto his front door was a note: COME TO CONEY ISLAND HOSPITAL AT ONCE. Dizzily, he spun around to see a woman running at him. "There was a fire," she rasped. "Your little girl was burned. Go quick!"

He hailed a cab and catapulted into the backseat. Was there always to be a fire? he wondered. Was what he feared always to hound him? He couldn't stop jabbering at the cabdriver. "He didn't know me from Adam," Woody would say, "but he talked to me and kept me from going to pieces."

He found Marjorie pressed against the emergency room window at the hospital. Three months pregnant with their second child, she fell back against her husband's chest. That morning, she sobbed, Cathy had worn her pink birthday dress. They'd walked together past the fun rides to visit Marjorie's parents. By afternoon, worrying that she wasn't getting enough vitamin C in her pregnancy, Marjorie had dashed across the street to a fruit stand. Cathy, so pretty in her pink ruffles, waited happily on the living-room couch, eager to answer the phone all by herself if it rang.

In the five minutes that passed before Marjorie returned with a bag of oranges, fire erupted in the apartment. Cathy was brought into the hallway, wrapped in a blanket, by a neighbor boy. Her skin was peeling away, her face was lumped into blisters. "Mommy," she whispered, "I burned up my new pink dress."

An ambulance took Cathy to the hospital. A fire truck pulled up in front of the building, disgorging men who dragged hoses inside. The Guthries would be told that a wire had shorted in a radio near the couch, igniting it. Cathy had tugged at the front door, but it was stuck, imprisoning her in an oven of flames.

Doctors asked Marjorie to sign a paper agreeing that she knew her child was "in a very low and critical condition." When Cathy was transferred to intensive care, Woody leaned over her bed, hardly believing his eyes . . . or ears. His beloved child, burned almost beyond recognition, began singing a few of his children's songs in a wispy, crackling voice. Her body was bandaged, but, almost jauntily, she waved a strip of medicated gauze at her "Pa."

That night family and friends gathered outside the hospital room. They took turns holding Cathy's foot upright so that a needle inserted there could quickly carry blood from hanging pint bottles into her veins. Sometimes she was quiet, sometimes she cried, but mostly she talked. She "called off the name of every person she had ever known," Woody would later say. She recited, like a chant, Woody's favorite nicknames for her: Miss Stackabones, Stacky, Cathy Bones, Cathy Rooney, and Stackarooney.

When Cathy slipped into a coma, Marjorie collapsed on a corridor bench, with Woody stretched across her lap. By morning the three doctors who'd hovered over the burned child brought the sad news to her parents as they stood, hand in hand, at the nurses' station: Cathy had died.

Self-portrait
by Woody Guthrie

It was Cisco Houston and Jimmy Longhi—the two friends who'd walked the decks of warships with Woody—who took him, hours later, out of the charred living room on Mermaid Avenue down to Coney Island's beach. Wind pounded their faces with sledgehammer force; snow covered the sand in crusty heaps. Woody walked stiffly, his eyes mostly closed. It seemed as if there were some ghastly stain over everything, never to be washed away: the deaths, by fire, of Clara Guthrie and Cathy Guthrie; the death, by disease, of Nora.

Woody suddenly fell onto the snow, arms and legs pummeling down to the wet sand underneath. Raw, agonized screams tore from his throat. Eventually the screaming merged with the crashing sounds of waves against the boardwalk. Then Woody lay mutely at Cisco's and Jimmy's feet, his silence making its own kind of noise.

When he finally got up, his lips were blue with cold. He began the walk back toward the houses edging the beach. It was all he could do right then. Somehow, he had to continue—even without his Cathy.

chapter NINE

I've been having some hard traveling,
I thought you knowed,
I've been having some hard traveling,
way down the road—
I've been doing some hard rambling,
hard drinking, hard gambling,
I've been hitting some hard traveling,
Lord.

—"HARD TRAVELING"

Coney Island along the waterfront, circa 1907

In the aftermath of his daughter's death, Woody holed up in the washed-down Mermaid Avenue apartment. With piles of condolence cards collecting on a table, he responded to everyone who'd expressed sympathy. His replies were multitudes of sentences memorializing Cathy. She'd been so "happy and creative," he wrote, and he composed a long poem for the boy upstairs who had wrapped Cathy in a blanket the day of the fire.

While Woody typed, Marjorie sat numb with guilt at having left Cathy alone for even a few minutes. She saw the misery in her husband's eyes. When the Bonneville Power Administration asked him to perform his Columbia River songs at the National

Rural Electric Cooperative Convention in Spokane, Washington, Marjorie urged him to go. She would be alone, but she'd focus on the new baby growing inside her.

In late April, Woody bought a train ticket to Chicago and Pampa. He visited his uncle Jeff and aunt Allene in Texas, where he reminisced about Jeff's teaching him guitar, then visited Roy and his wife, Ann. All of them talked of old times, helping to distract Woody from his sorrow over Cathy. Arriving by Greyhound bus in Spokane, he sang his Columbia River songs at the convention hall to thunderous applause. From there he hopped a freight to California and performed in Oakland and Los Angeles. His old singing partner, Lefty Lou, came to see him, now content at being a housewife.

Woody wrote letters to Marjorie, frequented bars, and had a meeting at Capitol Records about receiving royalties from recordings of his song "Oklahoma Hills." *People's World* wanted him to renew his lapsed column, but he couldn't work up the enthusiasm. He was tired and still had some trouble concentrating. He found himself tripping a couple of times and landing facedown on the pavement.

California was buzzing with reports of the HUAC (House Un-American Activities Committee). The HUAC was intent on ridding the country of Communists, real or imagined. Woody dispatched letters to several members of Congress, reminding them that freedom of belief was a cornerstone of the U.S. Constitution. In Los Angeles fear was rampant over blacklisting, the spreading censure that labeled people Communists, caused them to lose jobs, and cost them careers. Many Hollywood musicians, actors, comedians, dancers, and writers were, as Woody would explain, unfairly "black balled [*sic*], black listed [*sic*], [and] chalked up as . . . revolutionary bomb thrower[s]."

Though he felt somewhat nostalgic in his "re-doing" of California, Woody suddenly decided he wanted to go home. He canceled performance dates, returned the money, and slipped back to Coney Island, where Marjorie had been trying to rebuild their life. With funds borrowed from her parents, she'd made plans to open a dance studio where she could teach, while Woody sat down again at the typewriter. He'd decided to write a novel about his grandfather Jerry P. Guthrie's elusive silver mine, and he sent letters to Harry Truman, Attorney General Tom Clark, and Albert Einstein about the benefits of Communism and Socialism. He also wrote pages of erotic prose, sometimes mailing them to women he'd met. If Marjorie was bothered, she said little. Woody was just Woody—always off on some tangent.

In early summer eleven-year-old Teeny came to visit, and in July, Marjorie gave birth to a son who was named Arlo Davy. Woody and Marjorie would have two more children, a hedge against grief. Joady Ben (named after Woody's "Tom Joad") was born in December 1948, and Nora Lee arrived in January 1950.

Woody performed, though without his usual verve, at the People's Songs national convention in Chicago and for striking tobacco workers in North Carolina. He wrote a tender yet biting song, "Plane Wreck at Los Gatos (Deportees)," about the death, mostly ignored, of migrant workers deported to Mexico:

Goodbye to my Juan, goodbye Rosalita
Adios mis amigos, Jesus y Maria
You won't have a name when you ride the big airplane
All they will call you will be . . . deportees.

He spoke about his music on a New York radio broadcast at WNEW:

I hate a song that makes you think that you're not any good. I hate a song that makes you think that you are just born to lose. Bound to lose. No good to nobody. No good for nothing. Because you are either too old or too young or too fat or too slim or too ugly or too this or too that. . . . Songs that run you down or songs that make fun of you on account of your bad luck or hard traveling.

I am out to fight those kind of songs to my very last breath of air and my last drop of blood.

I am out to sing songs that will prove to you that this is your world and that if it has hit you pretty hard and knocked you for a dozen loops, no matter how hard it's run you down nor rolled over you, no matter what color, what size you are, how you are built, I am out to sing the songs that make you take pride in yourself and in your work. And the songs that I sing are made up for the most part by all sorts of folks just about like you.

By 1949, People's Songs had lost most of their bookings after supporting Henry Wallace, the Progressive Party candidate for U.S. president. Harry Truman won the election. American businessmen reflected the anti-Communist hysteria of the times by demanding that workers sign "loyalty oaths," vowing they were neither Socialists nor Communists. Blacklisting increased, leading Woody to write that he'd known "long ago that [his] songs and ballads would not get the hugs and kisses of the capitalistic 'experts.'"

That fall the black American baritone Paul Robeson—who'd pointed out that the USSR was the only nation to outlaw racial discrimination—was prevented from singing at an outdoor concert in Peekskill, New York. A mob had been screaming racial slurs at him and calling him a "Commie"; they'd destroyed his sound equipment and beaten up stage crew members (including a pregnant woman). When the concert was rescheduled and finally held despite threats made against Robeson's life, another mob gathered. This time, however, fifteen hundred union men from New York's Local 65 stood shoulder-to-shoulder in a huge, protective circle. Robeson gave a spectacular performance before an audience of twenty thousand. But as the mob started hurling rocks at cars leaving the field, and windows shattered, nearby police did nothing to stop the assault.

Pete Seeger, who had attended Robeson's concert with his family, wrote later that ten or fifteen rocks hit his car. He cemented three onto his fireplace as "mementos." Much "confusion, hardship, and misunderstanding" existed in the world, Pete would tell Woody, but making brave and fair choices could help people live in peace.

Woody's choices, so often brave and fair, were beginning to seem misguided. In one of his bouts of confusion, which were recurring more often, he mailed letters to Lefty Lou's sister, Mary Ruth, who'd written him that Jeff Guthrie had died of tuberculosis. Woody's letters turned sexual in tone, and, oddly, he sent her newspaper clippings of gruesome murders. Mary Ruth went to the U.S. attorney general in Los Angeles and, in September 1949, pressed charges against Woody for sending obscene material in the mail.

Jimmy Longhi, Woody's old friend and now a lawyer, took his case. In November, however, when the presiding New York judge asked thirty-seven-year-old Woody if he regretted sending the letters, he said that he had absolutely no regrets at all. The court, Woody declared, was acting like a blacklisting machine trying to smother his freedom of speech. The judge himself was equating sexuality with being a maniac. Nevertheless, Judge Harold Kennedy sentenced Woody to 180 days in jail.

It was Marjorie, eight months pregnant with Joady Ben, who

predicted that jail would be a playground rather than a punishment for Woody. On the road, jail had given him a warm bed at night if he couldn't find anything else. When he entered Manhattan's West Street Jail in early December, Woody had a ball organizing a musical Christmas pageant for the inmates. Rehearsals took place in the cells and in the guarded courtyard. But on December 22, Jimmy Longhi used his influence to spring his client.

Woody was furious. Couldn't he stay, he insisted, at least until Christmas? He and the inmates had a pageant to present! This time, however, he couldn't have his way. Yet, as he walked out of the West Street Jail his eyes suddenly went out of focus. He leaned against a wrought-iron fence, staring in shock as he saw his left arm convulse upward above his head. He remembered seeing such spasms before. Oh, yes . . . he certainly did. Not even the passage of more than twenty years could erase such a memory.

Woody shook his head. Impossible, he told himself. He'd be fine. Thrusting his body away from the fence, he walked over to Broome Street. He was going home to Marjorie and Arlo. The inmates at West Street Jail would just have to carry on without him.

As ice froze across the apartment windows Woody wrote the true story about three black brothers refused service at a Long Island café. But his songs weren't coming out the way they used to. Their rhythm and power were off-kilter. Songs he'd already written, however, kept him going. Pete Seeger and three other folk artists (Lee Hays, Fred Hellerman, and Ronnie Gilbert) had formed a new singing group, the Weavers, using some of Woody's songs. The Weavers' sound was mellower than the traditional folk music twang, making the group an instant hit with urban audiences. Their two-sided record of the Israeli folk song "Tzena, Tzena, Tzena" and Leadbelly's "Goodnight Irene" was a best-seller. They recorded Woody's "So Long, It's Been Good to Know You," which he had modernized for them. It rocketed onto the popular TV show, *The Hit Parade.*

In a letter to Mary Jo, Woody described how 125,000 copies of "So Long, It's Been Good to Know You" had been shipped out in ten days, with 25,000 copies of the sheet music printed. He received a $10,000 advance from Decca Records, and a new music publisher, Howie Richmond, released recordings of more of his songs, paying him a twenty-dollar-per-week advance against future royalties. He made a new friend, the Weavers' politically radical manager, Harold Leventhal, and gave Marjorie enough money to rent a bigger apartment.

By winter of 1951 Woody and Marjorie—with three-year-old Arlo, two-year-old Joady, and ten-month-old Nora—had moved to 59 Murdoch Court, across from Coney Island Hospital. Marjorie had trouble, however, persuading Woody to bathe or wear clean clothes. He'd grown a beard, was restless and moody, and stumbled over the children's toys, talking often of Cathy.

The apartment floor was strewn with empty liquor bottles. Many days Woody bolted into Howie Richmond's office, slumped into a chair, and spoke in bursts of words. Then he lapsed into silence. Howie was convinced that Woody had become an alcoholic, but it seemed a strange time in his life for this to happen. People who'd never listened to folk music knew of him. His songs were whistled, sung, or hummed on the streets. "This Land Is Your Land" and "Pastures of Plenty" were considered great works, and there was talk of "This Land Is Your Land" replacing "The Star-Spangled Banner" as America's national anthem.

Woody began wandering off again, hitching rides into towns where some of his relatives lived, knocking on their doors without notice. He often reeked so much of alcohol that, embarrassed, relatives sent him away. Marjorie was terribly worried, but she was also scared for the children. She even spoke of a loving divorce,

(left to right)
Nora, Joady,
Woody, and Arlo

telling Woody it might be best for all of them—but he wouldn't hear of it.

Occasionally Marjorie felt she had to kick him out of the apartment. He went to flophouses, from which he'd write her impassioned letters, promising to stop drinking. He was working, he said, on his silver-mine novel, which he now called *Seeds of Man*. If Marjorie would unwrap her heart, she would let "this crazy boy in just another time."

And, many times, she did. But when she looked at the scattered, stained pages of his writing, she was alarmed. He'd started putting unnecessary *y*'s in his words. *Afraid* became *fraidyful; bloodshed* became *bloodysheddery.* And he was signing his name *GOODY WUTHRIE.*

The drinking grew worse, and Marjorie finally had to ask Woody to please stay away. On New York City's Fourteenth Street he rented the same room where he'd lived when they first met. "Be my helping hand again," he wrote, but Marjorie knew he was not stable. When he had a ruptured appendix removed at Coney Island Hospital, she hoped he'd be put in a detox ward for alcoholics. Ensconced instead on the surgical floor, he handed out cigarettes brought by Howie Richmond's associate and made up rhymes about his nurses and medications.

After leaving Coney Island Hospital, Woody went on the run; he seemed to need comfort that liquor didn't provide. His legs began cramping up so tightly that sometimes he could hardly stand. He went south to Florida, popping in on an old friend, Stetson Kennedy, who lived in an abandoned bus at Beluthahatchee Swamp. He hitched rides into Okemah, where he wandered for several days down Main Street and to Schoolhouse Hill where the old gang house had been. "We [the gang] grew there," he'd once said. "Belonged there. . . . We were part of the roof, stove, spittoons, sacks, part of the scenery on that hill."

In New York again, he drove along the Belt Parkway with a young musician from Brooklyn, Buck Elliott (who would later be known as Ramblin' Jack Elliott). Buck played guitar and idolized Woody; he could mimic him perfectly, even down to his new lurching gait and slurred words.

In May 1958 Marjorie told Woody she was seeing another man: auto mechanic Tony Marra. Woody stormed into their Murdoch Court apartment, sent the baby-sitter home and the children to bed, and when she came home, attacked Marjorie with his fists. Terrified, she realized it was not really Woody hitting her. In all the years she'd known him, he'd never hurt a fly.

This was some crazed, demented creature. Breaking away from him, she called the police. Woody told them he'd go the next morning to sign himself into Kings County Hospital. Through the night Marjorie comforted him. "You're sick, Woody," she said. "And you promised you weren't drinking tonight. We have to find out what's wrong."

Over the next few months he went from hospital to hospital— Kings County, Bellevue, and Brooklyn State. He was on the detox floors and in the mental wards. Though he was evaluated physically and emotionally, and diagnosed as a possible schizophrenic or depressive with severe anxiety, the doctors were unsure what was wrong with him. They took his case history and learned of Nora Guthrie's Huntington's chorea, but the disease was rare, and they weren't very familiar with it.

Although Woody said Nora's illness wasn't hereditary, a doctor at Brooklyn State informed Marjorie that it could indeed be inherited. Originating in the nervous system, Huntington's chorea destroyed muscles and brain cells. Marjorie didn't give the information to Woody, as she didn't want to frighten him. But by the time another doctor made the diagnosis official, Woody had studied himself in secret at a mirror in the hospital washroom.

What he'd seen in the glass was the specter of his mother's face, with all its grimaces and tics. Her mouth had been twisted like his. Her eyes had been unfocused like his. And in that moment at the mirror, he *knew*. Past had become present. His drinking had only dulled the symptoms for a while. His attack on Marjorie, whom he loved to the core of his being, was a result of the uncontrollable tyranny of the disease.

He wasn't a quitter, he told himself—not unless he chose to be. He would meet Huntington's chorea on his own terms. In the waning days of that September, 1952, with his hands jerking and shaking, he wrote down the titles of four songs he wanted to create.

He would fight Huntington's chorea for another fifteen years, never quite able to compose those songs, but their titles spoke volumes about both his agony and his grit: *MY WORLD IS HELL,* he'd scribbled on a Brooklyn State envelope. *WHY DID IT HIT ME?, I WANTA GO HOME,* and finally, *A LITTLE FAITH.*

chapter TEN

There's a better world a-coming,
Wait and see, see, see.
There's a better world a-coming,
Wait and see.
Out of rumbling and of rattling,
Out of armies battling,
There's a better world a-coming,
Wait and see.

  —"BETTER WORLD"

Your own song is in your heart ...
yours is already ringing and singing
in your ears.

  —"HARD-HITTING SONGS FOR HARD-HIT PEOPLE"

The Bowery in New York City at night, 1942

𝓘n and out of the hospital, Woody stumbled now into his old haunts, much like Nora had stumbled through Okemah. He went to Bowery saloons, to Moe Asch's studio, or to food shops in Coney Island, trying to control his grimaces and shakes. Often he carried library books, and their chapters provided him some escape from the world.

Marjorie treated Woody with tenderness, almost as if he were a child, but she did not take him back. Doctors said his illness would continue causing erratic behavior, and she couldn't risk endangering Arlo, Joady, and Nora. Woody slept nights on friends' couches, though many of his old friends were gone. Alan Lomax was in England; Leadbelly had died in

1949; Cisco Houston was on the radio in California. As for Pete Seeger, he and the other Weavers were on tour. Will Geer was living outside Los Angeles on a Topanga Canyon compound—a creative fortress against the blacklisting in the entertainment industry. Recent Senate hearings to hunt down Communists had been chaired by Senator Joseph McCarthy of Wisconsin, a man who could ruin people's careers just by pointing his finger at them.

Woody, at loose ends, hitched rides out to Topanga Canyon, scribbling postcards to Marjorie from various towns along the way. Will Geer set him up in a cabin, showing off the compound's garden and the craggy outdoor amphitheater where the refugees from blacklisting performed Shakespearean plays and folk music hootenannies. Woody was greatly admired by everyone there. They weren't put off by his odd tics and garbled speech; after all, who could explain the artistic temperament?

Dizzy and wobbly, Woody spent hours at the community ceramic shed, lumping clay on a potter's wheel. Working beside him was a brown-haired young woman who seemed totally awed by his presence. Twenty-year-old Anneke Marshall was newly married, but when Woody—*the real Woody Guthrie of all those famous songs and union picket lines!*—asked her to take a walk with him, she left her clay behind and, in a short time, her marriage. Shut off from Marjorie and the children, Woody was happy to have a companion. With two hundred and fifty dollars wired from Howie Richmond's music publishing office in New York, he bought eight acres of cheap land atop a hill. But he didn't build anything there. In January 1953 he ran off with Anneke to New York, picked up Jack Elliott (the young man who idolized him), threw the disordered pages of his *Seeds of Man* novel in the backseat of Jack's car, and asked to be deposited at Stetson Kennedy's bus in Florida.

The next months slowly picked away at Woody's energy. Since they couldn't find Stetson anywhere, Woody, Anneke, and Jack decided to hang out in the bus. They arranged for Woody's royalty checks (about one hundred dollars per month) to be mailed from New York to nearby Jacksonville, but the cash didn't go far. Woody spent all day, with Jack keeping him company, writing meandering sentences for *Seeds of Man,* so Anneke—trudging down the steamy road—labored as a migrant worker on a farm. Still too awed at being Woody's "woman" to realize how ill he was, she beamed at discovering she was pregnant.

Excitement turned to panic, however, on the day Woody lit a match to a barbecue pit and the flaming gasoline ate up the skin on his right hand and arm. The burns were treated in Jacksonville but soon became infected. Distraught, Woody withdrew into his fogginess, not telling Anneke about the fiery curse that stalked his family. With his hand almost useless, he fled Florida with both Jack and Anneke. In Ciudad Juárez, Mexico, he got a quick divorce from Marjorie (who kept in frequent touch by mail), went back to Topanga Canyon, married Anneke in Los Angeles, and then returned to New York. Eight months pregnant, Anneke practically carried him into the dank, one-room apartment she had found on East Fifth Street.

New York was Woody's last stab at performing. Unable to pluck his guitar, he tried singing at hootenannies; but, disheveled and pale, he forgot his words. Moe Asch, who'd just released two albums of Woody's songs, was unbearably sad over what had struck down the greatest folk balladeer he'd known, the hillbilly genius dubbed "Shakespeare in overalls" by *Daily Worker* columnist Mike Gold. In the East Fifth Street apartment Woody played his old albums on a cheap phonograph or read books on Eastern philosophy. When Anneke went into labor on February 22, 1954, he couldn't get himself together enough to ride a bus with her to the hospital. He did manage to clean himself up for his new daughter's homecoming and drew cartoons on the walls to welcome Lorina Lynn Guthrie.

By summer Woody was even more disoriented. After an argument with Anneke he suddenly left. He made a final, valiant cross-country trek, riding freights he could barely climb onto. Groggy and uncertain on the road, he was arrested for vagrancy and spent more nights in jail. He turned up in Texas to see Matt Jennings, as well as Mary, Teeny, Sue, and Bill, then went north to visit his uncle Claude (who'd been the one to send Nora to the asylum). Everyone who saw him was aghast at his burned hand, his smelly clothes, and the dazed look on his face. On September 16, lurching out of a railroad yard in New York City, he checked himself back into Brooklyn State Hospital. He was forty-two years old.

In his hospital room, where Marjorie visited him every day, Woody read the Bible and sent cards in shaky, sometimes illegible handwriting to Anneke and his father. He befriended his fellow patients, unafraid of their delusions, ravings, and weird habits, cracking jokes for them and drawing cartoons. Soon he was the life of the ward. In one attempt at his old Coney Island Short Hauls, which he'd started compiling when Cathy was three years old, he wrote:

> Huntington's Chorea
> Means there's no help known
> In the science of medicine
> For me
> And all of you Choreanites like me
> Because all of my good nurses
> And all of my good medicine men
> And all of my good attenders
> All look at me and say
> By your words or by your looks
> Or maybe by your whispers
> There's just no hope

Nor not no treatments known
To cure me of my dizzy [*illegible*]
Called Chorea
Maybe Jesus can think
Up a cure of some kind.

Woody was eventually transferred to Greystone Park State Hospital (which he nicknamed "Gravestone"), a huge institution in Morris Plains, New Jersey. He arranged to spend weekends in East Orange with Bob Gleason and his wife, Sidsel, longtime fans, or with Marjorie (now married to Al Addeo, a carpenter) and the kids at their home in Howard Beach, New York. Marjorie knew that the children had a fifty-fifty chance of inheriting Huntington's chorea, but if they remained well, their own children and grandchildren would be safe. Marjorie tried keeping tabs on Lorina Lynn, but Anneke, who'd filed for divorce, had given her up for adoption to an elderly couple in Queens.

Friends, family, and adoring fans—including a young man and would-be folksinger from Minnesota named Robert Zimmerman (who, after he became famous, would be called Bob Dylan)—made pilgrimages to Greystone to visit Woody. Sometimes the Gleasons or Marjorie took him to concerts in New York City. On March 17, 1956, he sat in the balcony at Pythian Hall for a benefit concert in his honor. Many of his songs were performed, and excerpts from his writings were read. Brushing off hands that tried to steady him, he pulled himself upright, gritting his teeth against the trembling, as singers belted out the dramatic finale of "This Land Is Your Land." Cheering, the audience broke into tears.

Bound for Glory was published in paperback, and articles about Woody appeared in *Time, The Village Voice, The New York Post, The New York Times,* and many small magazines and music journals. People began to realize that they were slowly losing a national treasure. "A giant," wrote Robert Shelton of the *New York Times*, "in the form of a wispy little guitar picker, has been among us."

In 1960 Woody was present at a hootenanny bar mitzvah for thirteen-year-old Arlo. That same year, he read happily of the first Newport Folk Festival in Rhode Island, attended by 37,000 people. The McCarthy years of finger-pointing at possible Communists had quieted down, and the Bonneville Power Administration in Oregon named its substation after Woody. A trust fund, set up for his children, was earning about twenty-five thousand dollars per year in royalties, a collection of his Short Hauls (entitled *Born to Win* and decorated with some of his drawings and cartoons) was published, and Elektra Records put out a three-album set of his Library of Congress conversations with Alan Lomax. Folkways Records would later release 105 of his songs on four CDs.

By 1965 Woody could no longer speak, but could only point with a tremulous hand at "yes" or "no" cards that Marjorie held up for him. It was obvious to Marjorie, however, and to others who visited, that Woody had never allowed his illness to devour his spirit. Behind the ashen grimaces of his face was a steely, courageous intelligence, still holding on. And it held until October 3, 1967, when, unable to do more with his withered body than blink his eyes, fifty-five-year-old Woody hit the road again, this time into death.

(standing, left to right) Arlo Guthrie, Will Geer, Cisco Houston, Lee Hays, and Millard Lampbell. (seated, left to right) Woody, Nora Lee Guthrie, and Sonny Terry

At a memorial service given later at Carnegie Hall, Arlo Guthrie, Bob Dylan, Will Geer, Judy Collins, and a crowd of friends sang out a rousing, heartfelt version of an old protest song written by Woody for migrant workers he'd seen in their dilapidated camps: "I Ain't Got No Home in This World Anymore." In his own way, however, Woody had created a permanent home in the world for himself and his music, one that would withstand the fires of change.

At Marjorie's request Woody was cremated in Brooklyn, and his ashes were cast into the breakfront waters at Coney Island, his favorite spot, with Marjorie, Arlo, Joady, and Nora watching from shore. Major wire services and radio and TV stations carried detailed reports of his death. Airwaves filled with the sounds of his songs, and young folksingers who gathered on Sundays to perform in New York City's Washington Square Park raised their guitars that October in silent homage.

Marjorie would form the Committee to Combat Huntington's Disease (now called Huntington's Disease Association of America) to raise funds for research and to offer support services for patients' families. Having closed her dance studio to devote more time to the committee, Marjorie appeared in Washington, D.C., to speak about the need for improved diagnosis and treatment. Tireless to the end, she died in 1983.

A cure for Huntington's chorea (which in the year 2000 affected approximately thirty thousand Americans) has not yet been found, but various medications can quiet the symptoms. In 1993 scientists discovered the gene that causes the disease and created a test that can determine who carries it. Unfortunately, two of Woody's children, Teeny (Gwen) and Sue, also died in adulthood of Huntington's chorea. To compound the Guthrie tragedies, two other children—Bill and Lorina—were killed as young adults in automobile accidents. Charley Guthrie died alone in an Oklahoma City hotel room in 1956 but remained close to Woody until his death. Arlo (father of four), Nora (mother of two), and Joady (father of one) apparently have been spared by the disease, as were Woody's brothers, Roy and George, and his sister Mary Jo (who often speaks at schools about Woody). The former Mary Jennings, Woody's first wife, lives a busy life with her present husband in California. "I have no regrets about anything," Mary says, "except the deaths of my children."

Mary Jo Guthrie
(Edgmon)

In 1976 E. P. Dutton published a shortened version of Woody's novel, *Seeds of Man.* That same year United Artists released a movie version of *Bound for Glory.* Produced by Harold Leventhal and starring David Carradine, the film—which was nominated for Best Picture at the Academy Awards—deals with Woody's life in the late 1930s. A preview celebration was held at a Los Angeles theater, and the guest list included Mary (who had remarried), Marjorie, all the remaining Guthrie children, journalists from the U.S. and Europe, and hundreds of celebrities. Both Teeny and Sue were in the shaking stage of their illness but wanted to attend the festivities anyway.

The following year Ed Robbin, who'd remained a journalist in California, joined up with several singers to present readings and songs from Woody's work. Called *An Evening with Woody Guthrie,* the show was held once a month in Berkeley and San Francisco.

In the years since Woody's death, many tributes have been made to him. Dozens of singers have recorded his songs. "This Land Is Your Land," which was the theme song for George McGovern's 1972 presidential campaign, was recorded by (among others) Jim Croce, Paul Anka, Bing Crosby, Harry Belafonte, Country Joe McDonald,

Glenn Yarbrough, and Glen Campbell. In 1975 millions of school children throughout the U.S. sang the song at an appointed hour to open the annual Music in Our Schools Day.

Both Pampa and Okemah present annual tributes to Woody. In Pampa, not only has a highway been named Woody Guthrie Memorial Highway, but Harris Drugstore (where Woody worked) has become the Woody Guthrie Folk Music Center. Near Pampa's Civic Center stands an impressive musical sculpture in steel, 150 feet long and ten feet high, shaped into the notes to the chorus of "This Land is Your Land."

Each year starting on July 14, Woody's birthday, Okemah gives a three- to four-day Woody Guthrie folk festival held at the Crystal Theatre. Performing artists have included the Kingston Trio, Country Joe McDonald, Jackson Browne, Jimmy LaFave, Pete Seeger, Arlo Guthrie, and Larry Long; audiences have exceeded ten thousand people. In a small park not far from Woody Guthrie Street is a bronze statue of Woody that is surrounded by bricks, some engraved with names of family, friends, and admirers, others with personalized messages. A mural painted across the outside wall of an adjacent barbershop depicts important events in Woody's life.

Arlo Guthrie has become a highly successful singer-songwriter in his own right, a recording company owner (Rising Son Records), and a community organizer. His hit song "Alice's Restaurant" inspired the movie of the same name. Alice, Arlo's friend, lived in the old Trinity Church in

Bronze statue of Woody in Okemah.

A mural in Okemah on the wall of the hair salon, The Wright Kut.

Great Barrington, Massachusetts (its original structure destroyed, ironically, by fire), now home to Arlo's creation, the Guthrie Center, which offers art and music programs for children recovering from abuse. Joady, who lives in the Berkeley area of California, is an aspiring writer. Nora, a former professional dancer, is director (with Harold Leventhal as executive trustee) of the Woody Guthrie Foundation and Archives in New York, where many of Woody's writings (books, stories, poetry, letters), his drawings, paintings, and cartoons, his songs (more than a thousand), and a large collection of photographs can be viewed by the public. Some cartoons are on toilet paper or wrapping paper—whatever Woody had found nearby. On the Internet current Woody "happenings" are listed at *www.woodyguthrie.com.*

A traveling exhibition about Woody's life (sponsored by the Smithsonian Institution) opened in 1999 to rave reviews in Los Angeles and moved on in 2000 to New York City and Washington,

D.C., with plans to keep touring. In 1998 the U.S. Post Office issued a Woody Guthrie postage stamp. He was awarded, posthumously, Lifetime Achievement Awards by this country's Recording Academy in 1999 and, in 2000, the 42nd Annual Grammy Song Awards Committee, marking the cultural importance of folk music.

"Music," Woody said, "is just a handy way of telling what's on your mind." He never let himself be pigeonholed or buckled down. He never abandoned his convictions for dollar bills. He just walked out (sometimes when he should have stayed), went someplace else, came back when he wanted. Many young people, struggling for independence, collect his songs. They yearn, like Woody, to do their own thing.

In 1998, twenty million hungry people were still frequenting America's Food Banks, part of the welfare system for the needy. In 2001, 11.8 percent of the U. S. population was still living below the poverty level. Woody had been a down-and-out kid who formed a soft spot for the underdog and a rock-hard anger against oppressors. Loving the powerless, said Professor Richard B. Hughes of St. Edward's University in Texas, "is the most prized of Biblical virtues . . . [but] Woody Guthrie may be alone in history in writing a thousand songs for them."

Other folk artists, often modeling themselves after Woody, have carried on the folk tradition. Now called singer-songwriters, Bruce Springsteen, John Prine, Tom Paxton, Joan Baez, Bob Dylan (who, many say, comes the closest musically to being Woody's heir apparent), Pete Seeger, Arlo Guthrie, Joni Mitchell, John Mellencamp, Tracy Chapman, Bono of U2, Shawn Colvin, Ani DiFranco (who in the year 2000 created a recording tribute to Woody), Richard Fariña, and dozens of others have appeared at festivals such as Woodstock in 1994 and the yearly Newport Folk Festival, and in clubs and concert halls across the world. England's Billy Bragg, working with the Woody Guthrie Foundation and Archives, set some of

Woody's unpublished lyrics to music in two top-selling albums, *Mermaid Avenue,* released in 1998, and *Mermaid Avenue, Volume II,* released in 2000. In 2001, the story of Billy's project with Nora Guthrie to produce the Grammy-nominated *Mermaid* albums was released on DVD, *Man in the Sand (The Making of Mermaid Avenue).* "There's not a movement in popular culture," says Bragg, "that Woody didn't touch in some way—the beats, punk, the Beatles, even hip-hop."

In the twenty-first century, music schools teaching the "folk approach" or "folk-rock" (like Chicago's Old Town School of Folk Music) are proliferating. The fifteen hundred national members of People's Music Network for Songs of Freedom meet twice yearly to promote music that, like Woody's songs, can both rouse and aid the beleaguered. As writer Jody Rosen said in a July 2, 2000 article in the *New York Times,* Woody gave people "a liberating blast of the truth that they need."

Woody Guthrie believed in the equality and unity of all human

Joady, Nora, and Arlo

beings. His hope for a better world, where hard travelers like the workers can get a fair shake and a piece of the pie, still strikes a chord with us all. Woody just won't let us alone. In his song "Tom Joad," he tells us:

> Everybody might be just one big soul,
> Well, it looks that way to me.
> So wherever you look in the day or the night,
> That's where I'm gonna be, Ma,
> That's where I'm gonna be.

People will listen if you have
something to say,
but people will remember
if you sing it.

—HANSEN PUBLICATIONS

You find God in the church of your choice
You find Woody Guthrie in Brooklyn State Hospital
And though it's only my opinion
I may be right or wrong
You'll find them both
In Grand Canyon
Sundown

—BOB DYLAN

"LAST THOUGHTS ON WOODY GUTHRIE," 1963

⊸⊙ FAMILY TREE ⊙⊸

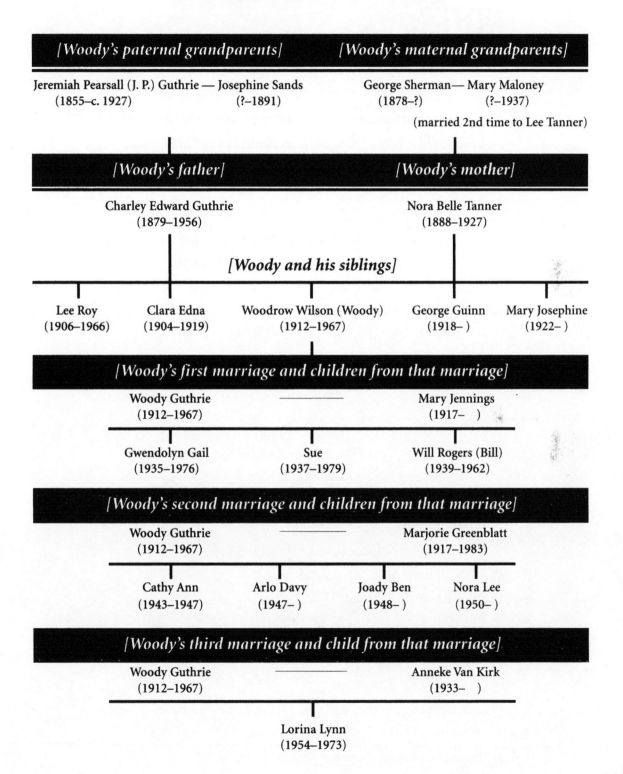

[Woody's paternal grandparents]

[Woody's maternal grandparents]

Jeremiah Pearsall (J. P.) Guthrie — Josephine Sands
(1855–c. 1927)   (?–1891)

George Sherman— Mary Maloney
(1878–?)   (?–1937)

(married 2nd time to Lee Tanner)

[Woody's father]

[Woody's mother]

Charley Edward Guthrie
(1879–1956)

Nora Belle Tanner
(1888–1927)

[Woody and his siblings]

| Lee Roy (1906–1966) | Clara Edna (1904–1919) | Woodrow Wilson (Woody) (1912–1967) | George Guinn (1918–) | Mary Josephine (1922–) |

[Woody's first marriage and children from that marriage]

Woody Guthrie
(1912–1967)   ———————   Mary Jennings
(1917–   )

| Gwendolyn Gail (1935–1976) | Sue (1937–1979) | Will Rogers (Bill) (1939–1962) |

[Woody's second marriage and children from that marriage]

Woody Guthrie
(1912–1967)   ———————   Marjorie Greenblatt
(1917–1983)

| Cathy Ann (1943–1947) | Arlo Davy (1947–) | Joady Ben (1948–) | Nora Lee (1950–) |

[Woody's third marriage and child from that marriage]

Woody Guthrie
(1912–1967)   ———————   Anneke Van Kirk
(1933–   )

Lorina Lynn
(1954–1973)

NOTES

CHAPTER ONE

p. 1 "squealing like a hundred mad elephants" Woody Guthrie, *Bound for Glory* (New York: Penguin Books, 1983), 86.

p. 2 "nice ripe and juicey [*sic*] strawberry" Dave Marsh and Harold Leventhal, eds., *Pastures of Plenty* (New York: HarperCollins, 1990), 177.

p. 2 "There never . . . streets." Dave Marsh and Harold Leventhal, *Pastures of Plenty* (New York: HarperCollins, 1990), 106.

p. 2 "all plainer" Marsh and Leventhal, eds., *Pastures of Plenty*, 160.

p. 2 "Let the wind . . . from!" Guthrie, *Bound for Glory*, 84.

p. 4 "Hello there, old *Mister Woodly*." Ibid., 134.

p. 4 "in a day or two" Ibid., 134.

p. 4 "Everybody's cryin' . . . out." Ibid., 134.

p. 4 "I know." Ibid., 134.

p. 4 "Woodly, don't you cry . . . Woodly." Ibid., 134.

p. 5 "a breaking point for my mother" Ibid., 135.

p. 5 "all twisted out of shape" Ibid., 137.

p. 5 "just like any other boy's mama" Ibid., 153.

p. 7 "looked like . . . us" Ibid., 138.

p. 7 "one or two sticks of furniture" Ibid., 138.

p. 8 "You done . . . it." Ibid., 140.

p. 8 "The world . . . them." Ibid., 140.

p. 8 "Home sweet home." Ibid., 143.

CHAPTER TWO

p. 11 "like a mole into everybody's trash heaps" Guthrie, *Bound for Glory*, 158.

p. 12 "half-kids and . . . half-men" Ibid., 158.

112

p. 14 "sprout and . . . again" Marsh and Leventhal, eds., *Pastures of Plenty*, 215.

p. 15 "It's your . . . died." Guthrie, *Bound for Glory*, 171.

p. 15 "by ear . . . playing" Jerry Silverman, *The Folksinger's Guitar Guide, Volume 2: An Advanced Instruction Manual* (New York: Oak Publications, 1982), 6.

p. 17 "Manhandled ya, egg scrambled ya, spondoolyzed ya." Woody Guthrie, *Born to Win,* ed. Robert Shelton (New York: Collier Books, 1967), 210.

p. 17 when Woody sang "When You Wore a Tulip" Joe Klein, *Woody Guthrie: A Life* (New York: Bantam Dell, 1999), 60.

p. 17 "take it easy" Marsh and Leventhal, eds., *Pastures of Plenty*, 45.

p. 17 "groovin' it . . . schemin' it" Guthrie, *Born to Win*, 211.

CHAPTER THREE

p. 18 "You just . . . twist." Guthrie, *Born to Win*, 143.

p. 20 "lasted a thousand years" Guthrie, *Bound for Glory*, 177.

p. 20 "fixed up . . . a hold." Guthrie, *Born to Win*, 146.

CHAPTER FOUR

p. 28 "I never . . . right." *Guthrie, Bound for Glory*, 178.

p. 30 "Well, I'm going." Klein, *Woody Guthrie*, 87.

p. 30 "Going. Where?" Ibid., 87.

p. 30 "California." Ibid., 87.

p. 30 "such a thick . . . not" Guthrie, *Bound for Glory*, 223.

p. 31 "good an' hot" Ibid., 23.

p. 31 "If it . . . them." Ibid., 195.

p. 31 "Git on outta town" Ibid., 214.

p. 33 "the nickel and the penny stages" Marsh and Leventhal, eds., *Pastures of Plenty*, 8.

p. 34 "Howdy. What's your name?" Guthrie, *Bound for Glory*, 253.

p. 34 "stuck in a tar pit of blind worries" Guthrie, *Born to Win*, 141.

p. 35 "we'll come . . . Washington." Guthrie, *Bound for Glory*, 253.

p. 35 "everywhere in . . . [there]" Guthrie, *Born to Win*, 69.

p. 35 "restless unrest" Ibid., 118.

p. 37 "His people . . . tie-coons . . . poly-tish-ens" (New York: Woody Guthrie Publications), 100.

p. 37 "that had a [lit-up] neon sign" Guthrie, *101 Woody Guthrie Songs, Including All the Songs from "Bound for Glory,"* (Los Angeles: United Artists, 1976), 100.

p. 37 "Sorry, got lost." Klein, *Woody Guthrie*, 102.

p. 38 "cotton pickers . . . workers" Marsh and Leventhal, eds., *Pastures of Plenty*, 7.

p. 39 "like a lost man getting found" Guthrie, *Born to Win*, 56.

CHAPTER FIVE

p. 42 "that was for a whole year" Marsh and Leventhal, eds., *Pastures of Plenty*, 8.

p. 42 "long tall . . . New England." Ibid., 9.

p. 42 "They made . . . singing." Ibid., 9.

p. 43 Based on an event where a female union organizer was stripped naked, beaten up, and hung from the rafters of a house. Klein, *Guthrie*, 168.

p. 44 "the rim . . . dump." Marsh and Leventhal, eds., *Pastures of Plenty*, 9.

p. 44 "all of whiskey" Ibid., 9.

p. 45 "For God's sake . . . please." Ibid., 31–32.

p. 45 "Hold the phone!" Klein, *Woody Guthrie*, 92.

p. 46 "as wide as your hand" Guthrie, *Bound for Glory*, 290.

p. 46 "This Rainbow Room . . . line!" Ibid., 292.

p. 46 "French peasant garb!" Ibid., 294.

p. 46 "No! . . . head!" Ibid., 294.

p. 46 "Imagine! . . . simplicity!" Ibid., 294.

p. 47 "hushed up . . . long" Ibid., 296.

p. 47 "not singing . . . it" Ibid., 296.

p. 47 "stock market . . . Wall Street" Ibid., 297.

p. 47 "fight and . . . power." Ibid., 299.

CHAPTER SIX

p. 50 "The enemy . . . sight." Guthrie, *Born to Win,* 163.

p. 50–51 "going like . . . slept." Ed Robbin, *Woody Guthrie and Me* (Berkeley, CA: Lancaster-Miller Publishers, 1979), 61.

p. 51 "to read . . . about" Marsh and Leventhal, eds., *Pastures of Plenty*, 9.

p. 51 "nothin' but . . . picker" Woody Guthrie, *Roll On Columbia: The Columbia River Collection,* ed. Bill Murlin (Bethlehem, PA: Sing Out Publications, 1991), 7.

p. 56 "sang before . . . workers." Marsh and Leventhal, eds., *Pastures of Plenty*, 10.

p. 56 "Our good . . . out." Guthrie, *Born to Win,* 73–74.

p. 56 "right out of the workers' lives" Klein, *Woody Guthrie,* 213.

p. 57 "She was . . . side." Marsh and Leventhal, eds., *Pastures of Plenty*, 11.

p. 57 "high rents . . . politicians" *101 Woody Guthrie Songs from Bound for Glory.* (New York: TRO/BIG 3), 101.

p. 58 "Now, Woody . . . this." Klein, *Woody Guthrie,* 236.

CHAPTER SEVEN

p. 60 "Love casts . . . all." Guthrie, *Born to Win,* 167.

p. 61 "pushed off the main road" Klein, *Woody Guthrie,* 262.

p. 61 "rebellious kid" *Woody Guthrie Publications.*

p. 62 "like [he] . . . out" Ibid., 251.

p. 62 "Music is . . . gun." Marsh and Leventhal, eds., *Pastures of Plenty*, 83.

p. 62 "wrecks, accidents . . . diseases" Guthrie, *Born to Win*, 72.

p. 63 "You can . . . songs." Marsh and Leventhal, eds., *Pastures of Plenty*, 64.

p. 64 "I am stormy . . . long waiters." Ibid., 104.

p. 64 "I have . . . comfortable." New York: Woody Guthrie Publications.

p. 64 "THIS MACHINE KILLS FASCISTS." Guthrie, *Roll On Columbia*, 7.

p. 64 "Howdy little Miss Cathy Ann." Klein, *Woody Guthrie*, 264.

p. 66 "A huge . . . life." Ibid., 267.

p. 66 "Woody is . . . poet." Ibid., 270.

p. 66 "Someday people . . . Yosemite." Ibid., 271.

p. 67 "It seems . . . does." Guthrie, *Born to Win*, 159.

p. 68 "Let's go!" Klein, *Woody Guthrie*, 288.

p. 69 "a full cargo of memories" Guthrie, *Born to Win*, 98.

CHAPTER EIGHT

p. 71 "He must . . . in!" Marsh and Leventhal, eds., *Pastures of Plenty*, 154.

p. 72 "I would . . . yours." Ibid., 145.

p. 72 "[He] saw . . . Birmingham." Ibid., 156.

p. 72 "I want . . . records." Klein, *Woody Guthrie*, 286.

p. 72 "So when . . . start?" Ibid., 286.

p. 73 "took us . . . sides." Marsh and Leventhal, eds., *Pastures of Plenty*, 11.

p. 74 "Everything is . . . hand." Ibid., 202.

p. 74 "make hoboes . . . us" Ibid., 164.

p. 74 "to band . . . together" Ibid., 204.

p. 75   "Daddy, why . . . time?" Ibid., 152–53.

p. 75   "Mommy, will . . . room?" Ibid., 152–53.

p. 77   "Let your . . . kids." Ibid., 178.

p. 77   "You're like . . . you!" New York: Woody Guthrie
Publications.

p. 77   "You give . . . ourselves!" Ibid.

p. 79   "social significance" and appeal to "the man on the back
street." Klein, *Woody Guthrie*, 301.

p. 79   COME TO CONEY ISLAND HOSPITAL AT ONCE! Guthrie, *Born to
Win*, 201.

p. 79   "There was . . . quick." Ibid., 201.

p. 79   "He didn't . . . pieces." Ibid., 201.

p. 79   "Mommy, I . . . dress." Ibid., 199.

p. 80   "in a . . . condition" Ibid., 200.

p. 80   "called off . . . known" Ibid., 200.

CHAPTER NINE

p. 83   "happy and creative" Klein, *Woody Guthrie*, 351.

p. 84   "black balled [*sic*] . . . thrower[s]" Marsh and Leventhal, eds.,
Pastures of Plenty, 197.

p. 86   "I hate a song . . . you." Guthrie, *Born to Win*, 223.

p. 86   "long ago . . . 'experts'" Marsh and Leventhal, eds., *Pastures
of Plenty*, 197.

p. 87   "mementos" Peter Seeger, *The Incompleat Folksinger*,
[Preface], ed. Jo Metcalf Schwartz (Lincoln: University of
Nebraska Press, 1992), 465.

p. 87   "confusion, hardship and misunderstanding" Ibid., 550.

p. 87   Based on Jimmy Longhi, Woody's old friend and now a
lawyer, taking on his case. Klein, *Woody Guthrie*, 359–60.

p. 90   "this crazy . . . time" Ibid., 383.

p. 91   "Be my helping hand again." Ibid., 386.

p. 91   "We [the gang] . . . hill." Marsh and Leventhal, eds. *Pastures of Plenty*, 215.

p. 92   "You're sick . . . wrong." Klein, *Woody Guthrie*, 388.

p. 93   "My World Is Hell," "I Wanta Go Home," "A Little Faith," "Why Did It Hit Me?" Ibid., 395.

CHAPTER TEN

p. 94   "Your own . . . ears." Marsh and Leventhal, eds., *Pastures of Plenty*, 65.

p. 97   "Shakespeare in overalls" Klein, *Woody Guthrie*, 149.

p. 98–99 "Huntington's Chorea . . . kind" Guthrie, *Born to Win*, 248.

p. 100 "A giant . . . us." Klein, *Woody Guthrie*, 450.

p. 105 "Music is . . . mind." Woody Guthrie, Written by Woody across a newspaper page (New York: Woody Guthrie Publications, circa 1940).

p. 105 "is the most prized . . . them" Richard B. Hughes, "Been Good to Know You: A Panhandle Town Comes to Terms with a Native Son," *Texas Observer*, 24 July 1992, 5.

p. 106 "There's not . . . hip-hop." Steven Mirkin, "Exile on Mermaid Avenue," on Launch Web site; www.launch.yahoo.com/read/feature.asp?contentID=157053; July 1, 1998.

p. 108 "People will . . . it." *50 Folk Songs of Today for Guitar.* Hansen Publications, quote from back-jacket panel.

INDEX

Printed in the United States
By Bookmasters